# WHERE MY LOYALTIES LIE: 3

## A Novel By
## KC MILLS

D1403564

© **2016**

Published by Leo Sullivan Presents
www.leolsullivan.com

# KC MILLS

# -1-

"Gotti, pick up. Please pick up." Najah could feel her heart racing. Forget racing, it was pounding so fiercely in her chest that she could feel it between her ears. She broke out in a slight sweat as she held her phone in her hand, on speaker, listening to it ring.

"Yo, do the damn thing." His recording came on, and hearing his voice made the situation worse. Not only did she have to worry about her brother, but Gotti was a part of that equation.

Not getting an answer, she sent a text: ***First and Prospect. It's a set up, the cops will be there, not Rah!!!***

After she hit send, she dialed again and waited.

*****

Gotti and Logic were inside the house looking around. It was big as hell, dark, and empty. The kitchen they were standing in was damn near the size of Logic's whole apartment, but it was set up like a typical trap location. Folding tables and chairs, no real furniture to speak of, but the house was functional. They both had their guns in hand, mindful of everything around them.

"Fuck," Gotti mumbled barely above a whisper when he felt his phone vibrate in his pocket. He glanced at Logic before he slid it out with his eyes on the screen, and then pressed ignore. He was about to shut it off when a text popped up and caught his attention. He read it from his home screen twice before he turned to Logic and whispered, "Let's go."

"The fuck you mean, 'let's go'?" Logic kept his voice low, but the irritation he felt was evident. He was damn sure hoping that Gotti wasn't bitchin' up on him. It was too late for a fucking change of heart about the situation.

"Trust me, we need to get out of here."

Gotti didn't know how Najah knew. He didn't know if it was true or not, but she knew where they were, and he damn sure didn't tell her. So for her to send a text with his location and that it was a setup meant something to him. He wasn't about to take any chances.

"Freeze, hands in the air, drop your weapon or I will blow your fucking brains out. Trust me, I don't give a fuck about policy or procedure."

Logic and Gotti looked at each other as they stood in the kitchen and heard a voice coming from the other part of the house. Neither of them hesitated as they turned to leave. There was no point in waiting to see what was going down a few feet away from them, but the second they hit the kitchen entrance there was a guy blocking it with a gun pointed at both of them.

"Got damn it." *This shit just couldn't get any better,* Logic thought.

"The fuck you think you're going?"

Gotti and Logic looked at each other and then back to the guy who was grinning at them like he was pleased with himself about something.

"Yo, you can shoot us if you want, but do that shit now because I'd rather go to the hospital than to jail. There's a fucking cop in this house a few feet away from us."

"There ain't no cop here. Moses sent me to handle whoever was left standing after you and Rah faced off, and since you didn't take care of Rah, then I guess I'll have to take care of both of you, or the three of you." He grinned at Gotti, adding him to the list of bodies that he planned to collect. "Put your fucking guns down."

"Aight, chill the fuck out."

Logic had a grin on his face as he held both hands in the air. He kept his finger on the trigger as he began to slowly kneel down like he was actually about to place his gun on the floor. Gotti kept his gun on the guy, but the second Logic's hand was roughly an inch away from the floor, he tilted his hand up and fired a shot that hit the guy between his legs.

He yelled and grabbed himself, unable to fire the gun he was holding. Thinking quick, Gotti fired one shot to the guy's head, causing his body to collapse and hit the floor. The two could hear someone calling out behind them, but they took off, not stopping until they reached Gotti's car and pulled off.

"The fuck was that shit?" Logic yelled, pissed off that within the past five minutes he had almost been shot and possibly at risk of being sent to jail.

"Yo, I don't fucking know, but your sister might."

Gotti pulled his phone out of his pocket, unlocked it and tossed it to Logic, who read the text.

"You told her where we were going?"

"Fuck no, why the hell would I do some dumb shit like that? But whoever did just saved our asses."

"This shit don't make sense, bruh. Why the fuck would Moses send the cops there and a hired gun to take us out, or me out. Shit, they didn't know your ass was gonna be there."

"The hell if I know. Where are we going?"

"My mother's house. I need to find out how the fuck my sister knew where we were."

"The cops had somebody hemmed up, who the fuck you think that was?"

Logic didn't bother answering Gotti. Right now he was more concerned about how Najah knew where they were. The two rode the rest of the way to his mother's house in silence. When they got there and stepped in the door, Najah ran to Logic and threw her arms around him.

"Oh my God, I thought you were going to jail."

"What the fuck is going on, Najah?"

She could tell from the look her brother displayed and the aggression in his voice that she needed to start explaining. "Nova was at work and some Alicia bitch and her sister were there. She messes with someone named Moses, who wanted her to send you to meet Rah and kill him, but the bitch had a change of heart since she was fucking both Rah and Moses. She didn't want you to kill Rah, so she decided to send the cops there instead. Nova heard the whole thing, and when she couldn't get you, she called me to get Gotti."

"And I'm going to find that bitch and fuck her up too," Nova said as soon as she walked in the door.

"You're not gonna do shit. Stay here, both of you. Until you hear from me, don't go anywhere," Logic demanded.

"Where are you going?"

"Don't worry about all that, just keep your ass here until I say so."

"Damn, you're welcome." Nova huffed and rolled her eyes.

Logic looked at his sister and cousin. He couldn't deny that they had likely saved him from going to jail, because if Najah hadn't sent the text, they would have kept moving through the house and possibly been seen by the cop or cops that where in there.

He stepped toward Nova and pulled her into a hug, but she kept her body stiff and didn't hug him back until he kissed her on the forehead.

"Thank you, but stay your ass here like I said." Logic glanced at her with a half-smile.

"Hello, what about me?" Najah said, eyeing Gotti and Logic.

"What about you?" He mugged his sister.

Najah rolled her eyes and Logic laughed.

"You're not on my watch anymore, my man got you." Logic nodded toward Gotti, who chuckled.

Najah grinned as he stepped to her before leaning down. He kissed her on the lips, and then said, "'Preciate you looking out, ma."

"Enough of that shit, let's roll."

Gotti ignored Logic and planted one more kiss on Najah's lips while Nova stood beside them with a huge grin. She was happy for her cousin, but still a little envious.

Logic and Gotti moved to the door, and just before they left, he offered one last warning. "Don't leave."

"Damn, we heard you the first hundred times. But look, when you're done, you think you can hook me up too? I mean, since we're keeping it in the family," Nova said.

"The fuck outta here with that. I didn't have shit to do with that bullshit." He narrowed his eyes at Najah, who laughed at her brother as she watched him leave and shut the door.

Once they were both in the car, Gotti started it up and turned to Logic. "Where to?"

"The hospital."

Logic couldn't get to Rah, but he could damn sure get to Moses.

When they reached the hospital, they parked and made their way to the front desk. Thanks to his team, he knew exactly what hospital

Moses was in and he had all of his information. Logic walked in and smiled at the girl behind the circular counter, knowing that she was interested. She had watched him from the second they entered the hospital lobby, and was grinning like a school girl.

"Excuse me, ma, I'm trying to locate my cousin. I was wondering if you can help me with that."

"I can help you with a lot of things." She winked at him and leaned back in her chair.

Logic could see Gotti out of the corner of his eye frowning and prayed that she didn't pay him any mind. By no means was she attractive. She was about six feet tall and couldn't have weighed more than a hundred pounds, which meant that she was a crack head type of skinny. She wore braids that should have come out months ago, and she had the type of bone structure in her face that should have belonged to a man. This prompted Logic to immediately check for an Adam's apple, and then look toward her hands. From his observation, he could tell his new friend was indeed a female who was just messed up and looked like a damn man.

"Oh yeah? Well, we might have to see about that, but check it. I need to know what room my cousin is in, and then I'll need a couple passes to get to him. Can you hook me up with that? He lost his cellphone before they brought him in, so I can't get a hold of him."

Logic's attempt to get the information they needed made Gotti walk away. He couldn't control the disgust that was surely plastered on his face and the laughter that was about to erupt.

She gave him that, 'yeah I can help you, but it's gonna cost you' look. "You sure it's your cousin you're trying to see?"

"Yeah, I promise."

"So what do I get out of this? I'm not supposed to give out room information. I'm supposed to call up and get you approved if you don't know the room number."

"How about you hit me with those digits?" He read her name tag before he continued. "Rona, and we can discuss what you get out of it later?" He also flashed her a smile. She blushed and melted. *Bingo!* He thought.

She leaned forward just a little to offer what he assumed what was supposed to be her sexy smile, but it had his damn stomach turning. "How about you give me your number, I try it while you're standing here, and then we can talk about what I get out of it later?"

*Fuck.* He didn't see that coming. "Aight, I can do that."

He rattled off the digits to his work line and she pulled out her phone and dialed it. He took his phone out of his pocket and held it up to her. It didn't mean he wasn't going to block her number later, but for now he had what he wanted.

"Okay then. What's your cousin's name, sexy?"

"Moses Tremble."

Logic glanced around and found Gotti behind him with a 'what the fuck' grin on his face. Logic couldn't look at him for long, or he was gonna start laughing so he turned back to his new friend.

"Umm, he ain't your cousin boo, because if he was, you would know he checked out a few hours ago. I'm sure he would have contacted you by now."

*Fuck.* "I guess he's been busy. 'Preciate ya, ma."

"Not yet, but you will."

Logic walked away shaking his head. Some people didn't have any fucking sense. She was smart enough to put that shit together about Moses, but not smart enough to realize he was about to block her number.

"Yo, he checked out. Head to the block, we need to find him. I know he's not gonna be at his place since I'm sure he's stressing about not getting confirmation that we're dead, but he ain't too damn smart. We need to find out where his girl is first. I bet he's there."

Once they were outside the hospital, Gotti stopped dead in his tracks and Logic looked back at him, trying to figure out why the hell he stopped. His crazy ass was just standing there grinning.

"What the hell is wrong with you?"

"Your little boyfriend in there is what's wrong with me. That shit was just wrong, Logic, and you know it."

Logic was trying his best to stay serious. With everything going on, he really needed to keep his head right, but Gotti was forcing him out of character.

"Shut the hell up and let's go. We got real shit to be worried about." Logic couldn't help but laugh as they made their way to Gotti's car.

Once they got in and were headed to the block, he looked at Logic serious as hell. "You're changing your number, right?"

"Why the fuck would I do that?"

"Because I don't want to have to explain to your girl why some dude in braids is calling your ass trying to get with you. You're on my watch right now."

Logic burst out laughing. "Yo, you're dumb as fuck, and that ain't right. But you know I already blocked that damn number, the fuck man? She would have been blowing my shit up. She's probably mad as hell right now because her text won't go through."

Gotti laughed. "You're right. She probably took her ass right to the bathroom and hit you up with a pic. With her Crypt Keeper looking ass."

"Man, shut the fuck up and drive so we can find Moses. Damn, you tripping."

Gotti was still laughing, but Logic ignored him. He needed to know who else was in the house at First and Prospect because whoever it was got arrested and he was damn sure hoping it wasn't Rah. He couldn't kill him if he was in lock up, and right now, Logic really wanted him dead. Fuck jail. Him and Moses both, and he needed that to happen real soon.

## -2-

"**Y**ou can sit here all night if you want, but nobody's coming to save you. I arrested you with seven hundred and fifty thousand dollars in cash, two unregistered firearms, and not to mention what else my team will find after they search the house. You can talk now or don't, I really don't give a fuck, but you're going to jail either way."

Rah looked at the detective sitting across from him and grilled him hard as hell. For some reason, his shiny bald head annoyed Rah as it beaded over with sweat. It was hot as hell in the interrogation room, but Rah kept his cool. He was irritated and wanted his one call so he could find a way to get out of there.

He knew he was fucked, but if he could somehow get out of there, he could kill Moses and disappear. Rah had money stashed at his crib, enough to get out of town and live comfortably for a minute until he could get set up somewhere else. He had a homeboy who lived in South Carolina, who got kicked out of school around the same time he did for selling dope on campus. He thought about hooking up with him. He had told Rah before he left to come check him out and maybe they could do business. That had Rah thinking about his current situation, and now was as good a time as any, because he damn sure wasn't about to do a bid. Was he gonna run? Hell yeah, if it meant freedom, but he had to get out of there first.

"And your ass can sit there all night if you want to, but I already told you I ain't saying shit. Let me get my one call so my lawyer can come get me out this bitch. You can't make me say shit, and I know my damn rights. I'll say two very important things one more time, and you're gonna get your tired ass up and make it happen, or I will sue the fuck out of this department." Rah looked right into Detective Nash's eyes and spoke slowly. "Phone call and lawyer. Now get the fuck out of my face until you're ready to make that shit happen."

When Rah finished speaking, he leaned back in his chair and propped his free arm up on it. The other was handcuffed to the table in front of him. With a grin on his face, he nodded to the door, further antagonizing Nash, who stood and slammed his fist down on the table.

"Look, I'm trying to help your ignorant ass. If you just tell me about Drew, then I can cut a deal with you. One year, maybe two, tops.

Otherwise, you're going away for a minimum of ten with your previous record."

"I don't know who the fuck Drew is, but I promise you this, I won't be doing one day of time, so fuck your offer." Rah wasn't about to make a deal by giving him information about Drew, not because he cared about snitching, but simply because he wanted out. If he made a deal, he knew he wasn't going anywhere.

Nash rushed Rah and grabbed his shirt in an attempt to jack him up, but Rah was a big man with muscle while Nash was about five feet even and fifty pounds over weight. He snarled as his nostrils flared, but Rah stayed calm. He wasn't about to react because he knew it would piss him off even more if he stayed calm. So he did just that. After another minute or so of a stare down, they heard a loud pounding on the window just before the door to the interrogation room opened.

"Nash, I need to see you." Another detective stepped into the room and eyed them both.

Nash let go of Rah with an attitude and stormed to the door.

Rah listened, just in case they said something that could help his case.

"He's not gonna talk. Let him make his call. There's no way he can get out of here, but Captain said we've had too many issues by not following procedure. If we get sued again that's your ass. So I suggest you do your job and let him make that damn call."

Rah grinned, knowing that he had won this round. Now, all that was left was for Marilyn to cooperate. She was his one call, and if she denied him, he was fucked. Marilyn was his only hope.

When Rah was finally granted his one phone call, he dialed Marilyn's cellphone and waited. It rang for what seemed like forever, and just when he felt like she wasn't going to answer, he heard her voice.

"What do you want Rahjee?" Her attitude boomed through the line.

"Before you say some dumb shit, just listen. I need your help. I know I don't have the right to ask you, but I am, so you'll either help or you won't, but I'm not gonna fucking beg."

As annoyed as she was, she was glad to hear from him, and knowing that he needed her made the situation even more enticing. But she was not going to let her true feelings about it show.

"Why would I help you? You don't need me, remember? Oh wait, your words were, don't call you, don't text you. I guess things didn't work out with Joy like you planned. From what I heard, she's pretty cozy with her new man."

"I'm not going to go back and forth with you. I'm in a messed up situation right now. If you're going to help then just do it without all the damn games, but like I said, I'm not gonna fucking beg you."

"Where are you?"

"Jail."

"Who's the arresting officer?"

"Nash."

"What do they have on you?

"Cash and unregistered weapons."

"Give me an hour."

Rah heard the phone click, so he knew that Marilyn had disconnected. As much shit as he was talking, she was his only hope, so he prayed that she could get him out of there.

"Alright, Tremble, let's go."

Rah's eyes narrowed at the detective as he grabbed his arm and shoved him toward the back of the precinct to the cage. Once he was inside, he eyed the man who was sitting across from him. He looked homeless and smelled like he hadn't bathed in years.

"You might as well get comfortable. You'll be moving in the morning, because aside from getting a call from the president, you're not getting out of here anytime soon. I don't care what your lawyer thinks.

"Oh yeah? We'll just see about that," Rah said with confidence.

He had no idea if Marilyn was going to get him out, but he damn sure wasn't about to let Nash know that he was worried about it. He took a seat on the bench across from who he hoped was just a temporary roommate. The old man had his eyes on Rah, which further pissed him off. The man just stared at him, but even though he didn't open his mouth once, just his presence alone irritated Rah. He didn't speak, likely because of Rah's size and demeanor. It was intimidating to most, even considering the fact that they were both locked behind bars.

Rah folded his arms and let his head fall back against the wall. He was ready to get out of there, find and kill his brother for setting him up, and then get the fuck out of Atlanta. He hoped Marilyn would come through, and he would be making moves soon. As much as he was aching to put a bullet in Logic's head too, it would have to wait. Right now, his first priority was getting out, killing Moses, and then leaving to secure his freedom.

*****

"I had to call in a lot of favors to make this happen. You owe me," Marilyn said as she and Rah left the police station.

Nash was fuming. His bald head and fat face were red as a beet when he had to sign off on the paperwork to release Rah. He even refused to get him out the cage once he was free to go, and instead sent a uniformed officer to do it.

Rah had a grin plastered on his face the entire time, even when Nash insisted that he would have him back in lock up before he could enjoy one night in his bed. This amused Rah more than anything because he had no intention of sleeping. His mission was to find and kill his brother, collect what little money he had in his safe at home, and then get the fuck out of town. The only problem he had with that plan was Logic. He wanted to see blood pouring from a hole in Logic's head so bad that he could barely focus. Rah was literally obsessing over it. The only feeling that was stronger was the urge to do the same to Moses.

And then there was Joy. He still wanted her. He didn't know if it was more about her wanting Logic, or the fact that he actually still had feelings for her, but either way, he couldn't remove the thoughts.

"Where are we going?" Rah glanced at Marilyn.

He was grateful that she got him out, but she annoyed the fuck out of him. He knew that she was going to want payment for her generosity, but fucking her was the last thing on his mind. She was also having to drive him to his house, which he knew meant that she was going to insist on coming in. He had to play nice, at least until he was able to get out of town, because his freedom was dependent on her.

"Briggs." He tossed out while scrolling through his messages. He had several from females, but nothing from Moses. Damn, nigga couldn't even pretend to care.

"I guess I should be flattered. After all these years, I finally get to see where you live," Marilyn said sarcastically, occasionally stealing glances at him as she drove.

As much as she wanted to be upset with him, she had to admit she was happy to be in his presence. She missed the feel of his body, which was evident in the fact that she called in some serious favors to get him out of jail. Favors that could affect her career.

Rah didn't say anything, he just looked up at her with no expression before letting his head rest on the back of the seat. When they reached his home, he took a chance to see if he could get away with ending things now.

"I appreciate you making that happen. You know I owe you for that shit." He leaned across the seat and kissed her. "I'll catch up with you soon. I have a few things to handle right now."

Marilyn laughed before reaching across the seat. Her hand quickly went to his lap and she gave him a nice tight squeeze. "Yes, you do owe me."

Rah inhaled, pulled the door handle, and got out, followed by an all too eager Marilyn. The second he hit his porch, he felt his pulse racing. His door was cracked, which meant that someone was, or had been in his house.

"Stay here."

He turned to Marilyn, who ignored him and followed him as he pushed the door open and began to cautiously look around. He no longer had a gun since they kept his when he got locked up. His first stop was the kitchen, where he pulled open the drawer where he kept a .9mm pistol. Rah had heat in every room of his house because he never knew when someone would try to catch him slipping.

After checking his house room by room with Marilyn's dumb ass on his heels the entire time, he was infuriated. He was almost hoping someone was in there and would shoot her so he could do what he needed to do without her breathing down his neck. After realizing his place was empty and it was just the two of them, his next thought was his safe. He rushed to the closet, and sure enough, it was wide open and empty. Moses and Joy were the only two who knew about it, and he knew got damn well that Joy hadn't been to his house

"Muthafucker!" he yelled before punching the wall.

Marilyn walked up to Rah, snaked her arms around his waist and began to unbuckle his jeans while she stood behind him grinning.

"Looks like you need me more than you think." She smiled, pleased with the fact that Rah was at her mercy.

He balled up his fist, knowing that he didn't have any other options. So when her hand moved into his boxers, he closed his eyes and didn't bother to stop her.

# -3-

Logic and Gotti were back on the block, sitting in the kitchen of their trap house. Gotti was in the process of rolling his second blunt while Logic had his hands folded behind his head, leaning back in a folding chair.

They were waiting for word from a few members of their team as to where Alicia lived. Both men were frustrated and ready to get their hands on him, but it was a little more difficult than they'd expected.

"Yo, we still don't know who else was in the house. We need to find that shit out. If it was Rah, that fucks up the plan. We can't body that nigga if he's behind bars," Gotti said randomly after he finished rolling his blunt and then fired it up.

"Yeah, I have somebody who might be able to help us figure that out. He used to be a detective."

Gotti looked at Logic with raised eyebrows and a concerned expression. "Yo, you fucking with cops?"

"Nah, nothing like that. He's cool, damn near family. You don't have to worry about him."

"Yo, a cop is a cop. Retired or not, unless they're dirty, you always need to worry about them. Hell, if they are dirty, you need to be extra careful," Gotti said with a certainty that came from experience before he took a pull from his blunt. He held the smoke in for a minute, and then let it go, creating a cloud in front of his face.

Logic chuckled at Gotti's distrust for cops. It was a must in their line of work, but Luther was the least of their worries. He had been retired for years now, but had held onto a few connections. Being a part of the system was one of the main reasons he'd fought so hard to keep Logic and his brother out of the streets. However, no matter how hard he tried, he quickly realized that he was fighting a losing battle, so instead he began to protect them. He did that until the day he retired and purchased Intrigued right after Bernard died. He offered Logic a buy in because he thought that would be the end to Logic being in the streets again, but Logic had killed Donte and Fezz. That one thing set in motion a series of events that changed everything. Not only was Logic back in the streets, but Luther no longer had the power to protect him.

"Nah, we're good. You'll just have to trust me on this one."

Gotti stared at him for a minute, as if trying to find his position on the matter, but then he eventually nodded to agree.

A few minutes later, Gotti and Logic both reached for their phones that were going off. Gotti's with a text from Najahj and Logic with a call from Joy. It was after ten, and he hadn't talked to her since he picked her up from work. He was actually surprised that she had waited this long to reach out.

"Where are you?"

He smiled at the sound of her voice. It did something to him every time. Even with all the chaos surrounding him right now, Joy's voice made it all seem so unimportant.

"I had a few things to take care of. What's up, you need something?"

"No well, you, but if you're busy…"

"I'm never too busy for you, Joy. You know that. I can't always drop what I'm doing, but you're my number one priority."

Logic looked up, forgetting that Gotti was only a few feet away from him, but Gotti was staring at his phone, apparently reading whatever message he had received. Logic stood and walked into the living room and sat down on the sofa.

"When are you coming home?"

Joy's question made him laugh. "Home?" he questioned.

This time Joy laughed just a little. "Yes, home. If I'm not mistaken, you made it clear that this was my home."

"Yeah, but we might have to find another spot since you put holes all in my shit." The vision of Joy in her bra and panties holding a gun, flashed through his head causing a reaction in his jeans.

"You me told to do it. So it's your fault." He could tell she was smiling.

"It's all good. That shit was sexy as fuck, though. I might need you to try that again when I get there."

"Well then, hurry up."

"I'll be there soon," he confirmed.

"I'll be waiting."

"Shit, you better be." Logic grinned at the thought.

After Joy ended the call, Logic decided to stay put for a minute, giving his body a chance to calm down. He grabbed and adjusted himself just before he leaned back and closed his eyes. Logic stayed that way until he heard Gotti's voice.

"Yo, we waiting this out? I just heard from Chevy and Roger. They still don't have any word on where Moses is."

"Nah, you can head out if you need to."

"I will, but I need to get shit right around here first. You heading home?" Gotti asked.

"Yeah. I'll hit you up in the morning, but if you hear anything, let me know."

"Aight, bet, you going to talk to your people?"

"Yeah, in the morning."

Logic stood and dapped Gotti before making his way to the front door. Just before he was about to step out, he looked back at Gotti. "Yo, you get my sister pregnant and Imma fuck you up."

"Gotti burst out laughing, but Logic was serious as hell. Gotti was his people, but Najah didn't need any more kids. Not right now anyway. As grown as she was, she was still his baby sister.

"Yo, I'm not going there with you, but I can say this, she's good with me. You don't have to question that."

Logic nodded and then left. He trusted Gotti, but trusting him with his sister was a whole different ball game, so for now, he would have to just see how it played out.

When Logic made it to his apartment he sat in his car for a minute to process everything. Once he went inside, it would be all about Joy, so he took a minute to mentally go over everything that had recently gone down, or at least he tried. Every time he stared at his front door, his mind drifted, knowing that she was inside waiting for him. Two of his fingers pressed against his lips because he could damn near taste hers just from thinking about them. The memory was just that strong for him. He smiled and laughed to himself when his first thought was his journal. The urge to jot down his thoughts of Joy flowed through his mind. He didn't understand it, but it made them more vivid, more real.

He climbed out of his car, locked the door, and then headed toward his apartment. He glanced around the area, mostly out of habit before entering, and as he locked the door, he could hear Joy moving behind him. When she was close enough, she wrapped her arms around his neck while he lifted her off the floor. Her legs locked at the ankles behind his back, while his hands moved under her butt to support her against his body.

"I guess that means you missed me too." She spoke against his lips before she kissed him in a way that let him know just how much she had really missed him.

"You smell good." He nuzzled his nose into her neck and inhaled what smelled like grapefruit.

Joy frowned. "You smell like smoke."

"Gotti," was all Logic said before he carefully guided her body to the floor after they entered his bedroom. He noticed the covers bunched up on her side and one of his journals on the pillow.

"What I tell you 'bout invading my privacy?" He grinned and nodded toward it before pulling his shirt over his head.

Joy climbed in bed and watched as he removed his clothes. Every inch of his body was enticing to her, and she was entranced every time he exposed it to her.

"What you said was, 'it's cool, I don't mind.'"

Joy grinned as she forced her body against the headboard, pulling the covers around her waist. She watched as he removed the rest of his clothes, and when he was down to just his boxers, she assumed he would wait until he was in the bathroom to remove them, but of course he peeled them off and tossed them on the hamper. He stood at the foot of the bed, arms folded, and continued his conversation like he hadn't just exposed his monstrous third leg that hung long and thick down his thigh. Joy tried her best to focus on his face, but it was a losing battle.

"So, you been reading that shit all night?" he asked with a smirk knowing that his naked body was distracting her.

"Yeah, why?" Joy managed to get out as her eyes moved to his waist and then back to his face.

"Come shower with me and show me what you learned."

"What?" Joy blushed.

"Those are my thoughts, things I want to do with you, things I want you to do to me, so come show me what you learned."

"No, stop playing." Joy blushed again but couldn't help but notice Logic's body reacting.

"I'm not playing, now bring your nosey ass on."

He winked and left the room. A few minutes later, Joy heard the shower. She debated on how serious he was for a few minutes before she finally crawled out of his bed. She had to admit, reading his thoughts had her damn near about to have an orgasm, just from his words, and she had helped herself to a few while she waited for him to get there. But her touch was nothing like she knew his to be.

The idea of turning his thoughts into her reality had her curious. Sex with Logic was always intense. He took his time with her, pleasing every inch of her body. Even when they got a little rough, he still managed to make her feel like it was more about her pleasure than his. She loved that about him. Something she had never experienced before. She had quickly become an addict.

When she pulled the curtain back, she watched as he dipped under the water, rinsing the soap away. Suds moved down his body, creating a pulsing between her legs as she watched. A smirk formed when he wiped his face and realized that she was standing there.

"Get in."

Joy removed her shirt, lifting it over her head and then stepped out of her shorts and panties. When she stepped inside, Logic wasted no time. He forced her back against the wall and slid his tongue in her mouth. One hand was firmly gripping her breast while he forced her legs apart with his other one and then began to rub her roughly in a way that had Joy's body on fire. His large hands covered her completely as his palm roughly rubbed across her clit. The combination of that sensation, his kiss, and the rotation of her nipple between his fingers was enough to send a mild wave of ecstasy through her body. Logic pulled away when he felt her tremble.

"Damn, Joy, I barely touched you," he said as he pressed his face to the side of hers, speaking into her ear.

Again, his hand was in motion between her legs, but this time he forced his fingers inside her. Joys body jumped and she tried to pull him away, but he leaned into her in a way that stopped Joy from moving, but still allowed him access.

"You don't want me to stop, do you Joy?"

Logic wore a cocky grin as he focused on her eyes. With no words, Joy shook her head to say no, so he leaned in and bit down on her neck. Sucking and biting her skin while he caressed her insides. After a warm flow dripped down his hand, confirmation that another orgasm had hit, he pulled her body into his.

Logic's throbbing erection was pressed into her stomach, creating a tortuous anticipation. The only thing he could think about was her mouth sliding down it. As many times as they'd had sex, Logic had tasted Joy almost every time, but she had never been down on him. As bad as he wanted it, he assumed she wasn't comfortable with it, so he never asked. Being inside her was enough, but right now he was throbbing and he wanted her to take care of it.

Logic took a chance, lifted her hand and placed it on him before looking her in the eyes.

"Show me what you learned," he said and looked down at her hands which were now moving up and down his length.

He had written several times about what it would feel like to have Joy's lips sliding up and down his manhood. At some point she had to have read it, or at least he was hoping that she had. Logic hadn't been with anyone but Joy since the day they first spent time together, so he hadn't had head since then. It had been months, and he was missing the feeling. Sex was one thing, but nothing could compare to the sensation of the warmth of a woman's mouth wrapped around a solid throbbing erection. He needed that from Joy, and even though he would survive if she didn't, it would damn sure make things better if she did.

Joy hesitated a little before lowering her body until she was on her knees, her hands continuing to move up and down his shaft. Once she was situated, she pulled him into her mouth, and the sensation was so damn strong that Logic almost nut right then and there. He didn't know if he was just missing the feeling or if it was because it was Joy, but he had to place his hand on the shower wall to stay on his feet as her lips glided down his length. The steaming hot water beating against his back while the warmth of Joy's month glided across his skin was doing something to him. Joy was giving him exactly what he was missing. He could tell that she wasn't experienced, but at this point he really didn't care. It felt so damn good to him, he would teach her the rest later.

When Logic felt his orgasm building, he began to force himself deeper into her mouth, and she handled it like a pro. With one hand on the wall to brace himself and the other balled up with a fist full of her hair, his head fell back and his eyes shut tight. He could envision her face in his head, and just before he exploded, he pulled her head back and covered himself with his hand. Joy watched as his body jerked, which caused his muscles to tighten and to flex.

Logic still had his eyes closed, but he could feel Joy watching him, which brought out a smile. After he got himself together, he reached for Joy and pulled her to her feet. He lifted her into the air with her legs around his waist. It only took him a minute to adjust before he was ready to enter her, and he did with so much force that Joy yelled out his name.

Her legs locked behind his back while he pressed her against the shower wall, and they two stayed just like that. Logic moved roughly in and out of Joy until they exploded together and were barely able to move. He lifted his head from Joy's neck, unable to control the smile he sported.

After a few pecks on the lips, her body slid down his and the two washed and got out. Once they were comfortable, Logic's arms wrapped around Joy. He relaxed and let his mind begin to settle.

"What's on your mind, Joy?"

"Nothing."

He pulled her closer into his body and kissed the top of her head. It was still a little damp from their shower, which made him smile from the memory of her mouth on him.

"Then why do you keep moving around like you can't get comfortable."

Joy didn't answer.

"Talk to me."

"That was my first time," she said.

Logic chuckled. "I know."

She lifted her head and frowned, assuming that she must not have done something right.

"Before you ask, it was perfect. Shit, I'm happy as hell that I was your first."

Joy laughed because his response eased the tension she was feeling.

"I'll teach you," Logic said randomly

Again, Joy lifted her head with a slight frown. "Teach me? I thought it was perfect."

Logic grabbed her around the waist and pulled her body on top of his. He kissed her lips before he spoke.

"Perfect for your first time, but I'll teach you how to be perfect for me all the time. Now stop pouting and take your ass to sleep. You know them bad ass kids are gon' have you running, and that colorful ass room is gon' have your head spinning."

Joy sucked her teeth and let her head rest on his shoulder. She wasn't about to go back and forth with him about her kids, plus she was tired. So as he moved his hand up and down her back, gliding across her skin, she closed her eyes and focused on his heartbeat. Before she knew it, she was out.

# -4-

Logic looked down at his mother and frowned when she opened Luther's door. She was dressed in something that she appeared to have slept in, which didn't sit right with him.

"Did you stay here last night?"

Mini laughed at her son so called having a problem with her staying overnight with Luther.

"Are you coming in or you want me to get Luther for you? I assume you're here to see him since that dumb ass look on your face lets me know you weren't expecting to see me."

Logic watched as his mother let go of the door and stepped aside so that he could step in.

"Did you?" he asked after he shut the door behind him.

"It's ten o'clock in the morning, Auggie, what do you think?"

"Yo, Ma, really?"

It irked him even more when she laughed it off. No son wants to think about their mother being with a man. No matter how grown they were. Out of sight out of mind, but standing here in front of her made it hard to ignore.

"Boy, I'm grown. How the hell do you think you got here? The same way I didn't say shit about you laying up in my house with Joy, you won't say a damn thing about me being with Luther.

"First of all, I don't want to hear that shit, and second of all, I didn't do anything in your house, so that's different. I wouldn't disrespect your house like that, Ma. Damn."

Again, Mini laughed. "Well, this ain't your house. Let's just leave it at that. I bet you better stop turning your face up at me like that too."

Logic tucked his lip between his teeth and clenched his jaw before shaking his head when he watched his mother walk down the hall in the direction of what he knew was Luther's bedroom. As a kid, Logic had spent a lot of time at Luther's house since he was the only real male figure in his life.

"Morning, son, your mother said you needed to talk to me." Luther stepped to Logic and pulled him into a hug before he moved past him in route to the kitchen.

Logic followed him and sat down at the table positioned in the corner.

"When I said take care of my mother, that damn sure ain't what I meant," Logic said, pointing toward the back of the house where he knew his mother was.

Luther chuckled. "You don't get to have it both ways, but at least you know that she's in good hands."

Luther opened his refrigerator and began removing what looked like breakfast items.

*This nigga is making breakfast.* Logic was irritated to know that his mother was the inspiration behind it. Even when they were kids, Luther didn't cook. When Luther spent time with him, his brother, and Najah, he would always take them out to eat.

Getting his thoughts together, he focused on the reason he was there. "You still in touch with people at 57?"

Luther turned to face Logic at the mention of his old precinct. "A few, yeah. Why?"

"I need to find out the name of someone who was arrested last night."

Logic waited, knowing that Luther wouldn't be thrilled about him checking into something like that.

"I can make a few calls, but do I need to?"

Luther's question was not as simple as it sounded, but Logic saw right through it and explained as best he could without really telling Luther what he knew.

"I'm trying to locate somebody. If it was them who got knocked, then I can stop searching."

Luther stared at Logic for what seemed like forever, not really knowing if he wanted to commit to helping. Finding out the information that Logic was asking for could cost someone their life and he knew that. Just as he was about to respond, Mini walked into the kitchen. She made her way over to Luther, sensing that she had walked in on something. Luther pulled her small body to his tall frame before leaning down to kiss her.

Her eyes moved from her son to Luther in a suspicious manner before she addressed Luther.

"I got this. I'm really not in the mood to be calling the fire department today," she said and then playfully shoved him out the way.

Luther chuckled. "I'm not that bad."

Logic couldn't help but appreciate the way his mother was beaming. She was happy, and if Luther was the reason for that, then he would figure out how to be okay with their relationship. Technically, he already was, it was just going to take some getting used to.

"I'll make some calls," Luther said after sitting down across from Logic.

"Calls about what?" Mini questioned, peering at them both.

"You worry about that and let me worry about this," Luther said playfully, which caused Mini to roll her eyes.

"Aight, I appreciate that."

"You staying for breakfast?"

"No." Mini yelled from inside the refrigerator, causing both of them to laugh.

"Damn, Ma, it's like that?"

"Just like that," she said after removing a carton of eggs and setting them on the counter.

"Yo, I got shit to do anyway. I'm out." He stood, walked over to his mother and kissed her on the cheek before leaving the kitchen.

"Bye, baby. I love you." She yelled behind him after he was out the kitchen.

Luther followed Logic to the door, laughing to himself about how bipolar Mini could be. Pissed one minute and then all lovey dovey the next.

"What do I need to know?"

"First and Prospect. Just find out who they took down. That's all I need to know."

"Is your name gonna come up?" Luther needed to be prepared for whatever he was going to be faced with when he started asking questions.

"Nah, it shouldn't. I wasn't there."

Luther inhaled and released it slow. "Alright, I'll give you a call in a few hours. You good? Everything good?"

"I will be soon enough," Logic admitted.

Once Logic found out if Rah was the one arrested and his people located Moses, shit would be lovely. But for now, it was a waiting game.

Luther nodded and Logic left. He needed to head to the block and check in with Gotti. Hopefully, somebody had word on Moses, or at least where Alicia lived.

*****

"Hold up, ma, I need to get this." Gotti stepped away from Najah to answer the incoming call from Logic. He held his phone to his ear while he puffed on the freshly rolled kush he had in his hand.

Najah sat patiently waiting for him on his bed while she surveyed his room. *Gotti is the complete opposite of my brother,* she thought as he looked around. Gotti had piles of clothes everywhere. Things were scattered all over his dresser, and nothing seemed to be in place. His bed, which she was sitting on, wasn't even made, but she could tell the sheets were clean. She had given them a thorough inspection when he left her alone to use the bathroom.

Najah refused sit on a bed that he'd had some other female on. His apartment wasn't necessarily nasty, just sort of disheveled. In need of a woman's touch, she decided as her eyes continued to roam while he talked on the phone. The only thing that had any organization was the neatly stacked boxes of shoes that lined one wall damn near equivalent to the height and length of the dresser that they shared the wall with. Najah grinned, knowing that Gotti had an obsession with shoes. Every time she was around him he was in a different pair, all equally expensive and some special editions.

The fact that Gotti turned his back to her and answered the call, but didn't leave the room made her roll her eyes because she could still eavesdrop if she wanted to. Najah, however, had no interest in their street business as long as they were both safe.

"What's up, did you find out anything?"

"Nah, not yet, but he's going to make some calls. We should know something in a few hours. What's business looking like?"

Gotti glanced over his shoulder at Najah. "Shit is straight. I just left from out there. I'm about to chill for a minute and then head back."

Logic laughed. Gotti was always about business, so if he wasn't on the block there was only one reason why. "Tell my sister I said what's up and she better be back in time to get Trent. I'm serious as fuck, yo, don't get my sister pregnant or I'm fucking both of y'all up."

Gotti looked at Najah again and laughed. "I got this shit, you just worry about finding Rah and Moses so we can body them niggas."

"What the fuck ever. I'm serious about that shit."

"Yo, I'm out. Hit me when you find out something."

Gotti placed his phone on the table next to his bed, then stood next to it a few feet away from where Najah was sitting on the foot of his bed staring back at him. His eyes traced her body through the cloud of smoke that he released, and as he did, a grin started to surface.

"He knows I'm here?" Najah asked as she returned Gotti's stare.

"Yeah, why?"

She shrugged. "No reason."

"He said make sure you get home in time to get your shorty, and I better not get you pregnant."

Najah's eyes stretched wide. "He did not."

She was embarrassed by Logic saying something so crazy, but not surprised by it at all. He was just like that. As embarrassed as she was, though, the only thing she could think about right now was how sexy Gotti would look with his clothes off. She didn't want him to get the wrong idea, so she didn't vocalize it.

Logic telling him not to get her pregnant insinuated that Gotti could have sex with her. She wanted to because she couldn't get over how sexy he was, but she damn sure didn't want him to think she was easy. She really wasn't. Fezz had been the only man that she had ever been with, and that was a lot of the reason she kept going back. She was a firm believer that your first would always have a hold on you.

Fezz was gone, thanks to Logic, and after the way he'd treated her, she couldn't say she was upset about it. But she damn sure missed some parts of him. Being around Gotti was not making it any better.

"He did, and it's not the first time he said that shit either. But you grown, right?"

"Yeah, but I'm not easy if that's what you're thinking."

"What do you consider easy?"

"That I would just sleep with anybody."

"Having sex with somebody you feeling don't make you easy, ma. It just means you want what you want. It's all about choices. If you want to have sex with me, which clearly you do, then why shouldn't you? I'm feeling the fuck outta you, and I hope we about to make something out of this. But for the record, I know you not a hoe or no shit like that. I know you've only been with Fezz, or at least that's what I assume."

"What makes you so sure?"

"Because if you were a hoe, I wouldn't be making moves to put you on my team. I would have fucked you the first night at your mom's crib and kept it moving. You damn sure wouldn't be up in my spot where I lay my head. Some shit you just know, and I know you don't get down like that."

"Who says I want to have sex with you?" Najah folded her arms defensively across her chest. Even if it was true, he had no right to call her on it. Was she that easy to read?

"You said it. Your eyes, the way you keep looking at me. You struggling over there, ma, but it's cool. I want you too. Just not yet. I told you. You need to be sure I'm what you want, because once I hit that and you fucking with me on some real shit, there won't be no back and forth. You'll be mine. This ain't nothing to play with."

Gotti's eyes moved down his chest and stopped at his waist before he looked Najah's way again and then winked at her. She blushed but didn't say anything because she was at a loss. Gotti was so straightforward and different from Fezz. She wasn't used to it, but she liked it.

"You don't like to clean, I see." She decided to take the heat off her and change the subject.

Gotti put his blunt out on the ash tray next to his bed and then sat down next to her. He knew what she was doing, but he decided to let her have it.

"I clean when I need to, but I'm never here. I'm always on the block. That's probably how your brother knew I was with you. I'm usually on the block night and day, but my shit isn't nasty. There are no dirty dishes in my sink or trash anywhere, and my bathroom is clean. Aside from the fact that my bed isn't made and there are a few piles of clothes, my shit is straight. Why the fuck would I make my bed when I'm gonna get right back in it?"

He grinned at Najah before he pulled her to him. He lifted her with ease onto his lap facing him. She was now straddling his waist and watching him. Gotti's hands gripped her tiny waist before they moved up her back, and then back down her sides where he grasped the hem of the shirt she was wearing and pulled it over her head. He stared at her apple sized breasts before he bit his bottom lip and then kissed her neck.

"I thought you said I had to wait."

Gotti chuckled. "You do. I'm not about to have sex with you. I just wanted to see your body. You're little as fuck. Your damn son is gonna be as tall as you in a minute." Gotti let his hands move across her stomach.

"Why don't you have stretch marks? I thought all women had those after they had a baby."

She shrugged before looking down to where his hands were on her stomach. He was still inspecting her mid-section, so he wasn't looking at her.

"I just don't. I guess I was lucky. I carried small, though. You couldn't even really tell I was pregnant with Trent until I was almost six months."

Gotti chuckled before he looked in her eyes and then pulled her body close to his and kissed her. Najah melted into his kiss. His lips were so soft and his kiss was so gentle, even though he was damn near double her size and holding her body roughly against his.

"You sure I have to wait?" Najah said and glanced down toward where their bodies connected. She could feel him growing beneath her.

"I didn't say that I didn't want you, I just said that you had to wait. I need to make sure you're ready before I give you all this."

Najah rolled her eyes, which made him laugh. He was serious though. He knew what he was working with, and he wasn't about to have her strung out until he knew she had her head right.

"So what's up wit' your shorty? He seems like a good little dude."

Gotti reached for the top of his bed and grabbed a pillow. After positioning it under his head, he leaned back until his head rest comfortably on it. His hands continued to move across Najah's skin, even moving under her bra and caressing her breasts. His touch was driving Najah insane and making it extremely hard for her to focus, but she fought through it.

"What's there to say? He's my baby. He's a hardheaded ass boy, and I see so much of his father in him. Too much, in fact. So much so that I really can't stand to look at him sometimes, but he's a good kid. Thank goodness for my brother because he keeps Trent in line. I don't know, I guess my son is my heart."

"I like the fact that you're a real mom. I respect that. I see too many females who have kids and don't do shit with them or for them."

"Well, that's not me. I love my son."

"I feel you."

"What about you?"

"What about me?" Gotti's eyes were on her body again and he was currently unbuckling her belt.

"Do you have kids?"

A smirk spread across his face, but he kept his eyes on what he was doing, which was unbuttoning her jeans and then unzipping them. Once he had them open, he pulled the fabric farther apart and let his fingers glide across the skin above her panty line. Because it was such a sensitive area, Najah flinched, but kept her cool. She was struggling and on the verge of losing it, but she fought back the moan that was sitting in her throat and kept silent.

"Nah, not yet, but I want some, just with the right person."

His eyes connected with hers for a second and then went right back to the skin that he had exposed from unbuttoning her jeans.

"The right person, huh?"

Najah's breathing picked up a little because Gotti now had his fingers inside her jeans. They weren't inside her, just rubbing against the thin material of her panties that covered her center.

"You alright, ma?"

Gotti grinned, knowing exactly what he was doing. He watched her face change, which caused him to grow even harder beneath her, but Gotti had control. He just wanted to touch her body. He wasn't going to try to have sex with her, not yet. Gotti meant what he said about her being ready, and he'd had sex that morning with a shorty he was messing around with. She wasn't anybody serious, but he wasn't about to disrespect Najah by sliding in her after he had been with someone else.

"I'm fine."

Najah leaned back just a little, placing her hands behind her on Gotti's legs. She was fighting hard to hold onto the orgasm that was building in her because she didn't want him to know just how badly he was affecting her. It had been a minute since she had been that close to or handled by a man, so Gotti was really pushing her over the edge. It didn't last long, though, because out of nowhere he ended it. Just like that, he stopped.

He removed his hand, began fastening her jeans and then handed her shirt to her. "Come on, let's roll. I wanna grab something to eat. What time do you have to pick your shorty up from school?"

Najah grabbed her shirt, turned it the right way, and then pulled it over her head. She stared at Gotti, almost upset that he had her feeling so good and then just shut it off, but she kept it to herself.

She didn't have to say anything because it was written all over her face.

"Three fifteen," she said, and tried to lift her body from his, but he grabbed her and held her in place.

"You mad?" The smirk he wore made it worse.

"About what?" Her stare was deadly, which made him smile harder.

"Nothing, let's go. We can eat, and then I'll take you to get Trent."

He stood and lifted her from his lap. After he grabbed his phone and keys, they left his apartment. Once they were in his car and heading to eat, Gotti placed his hand on her leg and glanced at Najah for a second. She was quiet and he knew why.

"Next time, just ask for what you want and I'll give it to you, instead of pouting about it. But don't worry, ma, I'll make you cum soon enough. Just be patient."

He turned her way and waited for her to look at him. She fought against it for as long as she could, but eventually she broke. When she did, he winked at her and then chuckled. As mad as Najah was, he had her feeling some type of way and she liked it. She had a feeling that Gotti was about to change her world.

# -5-

Mini moved around Luther's kitchen pretending to be busy. She had followed him out the bedroom and was now hovering, trying to find out what he was doing. The phone call he'd made to his old precinct had something to do with Logic, and as much as she wanted to pretend that she didn't care, she couldn't help but wonder what he was into. So she listened to Luther's end of the conversation, trying to make sense of the situation.

"Rah Tremble? What was the charge?... So with a record and that much cash, his lawyer got him out? Who the hell was his lawyer, God?... She must have called in some serious favors. Yeah, I appreciate it. Take care... you too."

Luther ended the call and looked right at Mini. He knew that she was listening and he didn't want to have a conversation with her about what Logic was into. It wasn't a secret, but that didn't mean he wanted to actually discuss it with her.

"What's that about?" she asked, eyes focused on him, arms folded across her chest, looking like she was about to handle somebody. Mini was tough, but she had no give with Luther, and she knew it.

"Don't do that. The more you know, the more you worry. It was nothing, and he's fine." Luther placed his phone on the counter before walking over to kiss Mini's cheek.

"I know that name. Rah is the man Auggie almost shot in my house, so if you're making calls to find out information about him, then it's something."

"I'm not going to have this conversation with you, Mini," Luther said firmly and he meant it.

"That's my son, Luther."

"You don't think I know that? Hell, he's just as much my son as he is yours."

"Then don't act like I don't have the right to be worried about him."

"I'm not saying you can't worry, but what I am saying is that he made his choice. You worrying won't change that."

Mini stood there watching him. Not saying a word. She was upset, but couldn't find the proper words to express it.

"Look, you and I decided a long time ago not to let these kids come between what we have, and we're sticking to that. I promised you to keep him safe as much as I can, and I'm doing that. In the streets and from you, if necessary."

"Me?" She pointed to her chest, looking surprised.

"Yes, you, Mini. He needs to have his mind right while he's out there. That's the first step to him being safe, so that means he can't worry about things that might cloud his judgment, things like worrying about you. If he's worried about you, then he can't focus on what he needs to focus on to stay safe. So, yes, I'm protecting him from you by keeping you as far away from this situation as possible. That's my son too, Mini. You know that, and I don't love the choice he made, but it was his to make. I will do anything I can to make sure he lives another day. I need you to trust me on that."

Luther's hands caressed the sides of Mini's face lovingly before he kissed her again. She knew that he was right, and as much as she hated it, she had to let it go.

"You're right. It's just hard. My babies are everything to me. You know that."

Luther smiled as he grabbed Mini's hand and led her to the living room. He sat down and then pulled her into his lap. Once she was comfortable, he spoke.

"They're not babies anymore, and they have to be responsible for the choices that they make. Najah, Augustus, and even Nova. You can't save them from themselves, Mini. They're good kids. You raised them right. They're all going to be fine, but right now it's time for you to focus on you. I need you to focus on us."

Mini smiled as she looked up at Luther's handsome face. She loved this man with everything she was. His salt and pepper hair was cut low to his head and matched the neatly trimmed mustache and goatee that adorned his face. His almond shaped dark eyes where welcoming to her, the way they always stared intensely into her soul. At fifty-six years old, Luther was still very sexy to her. Not perfect, but in great shape for his age. In fact, aside from a barely noticeable mid-section, he was quite fit. His chest and arms where nicely defined as she leaned against their firmness and his arms circled her body. Luther was most definitely easy on the eyes.

What made it even better was that he had a heart of gold. He was such a loving and caring man, even when she refused to accept it. For years, she'd kept her distance. Mostly because her focus was on her children, but after losing her son, she realized that life was short and she had to live. That was the only good thing that had come from the situation. After years of fighting against it, she had finally given in to Luther's advances and decided to give him a chance. Hell, he had been there for her when no one else had. He gave her a job and sold her the home they lived in now for far less than she knew it was worth. He helped her start the business she owns now, and most importantly, he had been a father to her children when their own had refused to do so.

After Mini left New York for Atlanta and got clean, she had contacted Hoover and made it clear that he would never be a part of her life again, but that he could be a father to his children. She remembered making the call as she sat at her kitchen table with Luther next to her, rubbing her back for support, even after he tried to convince her that it was a terrible idea.

Hoover had laughed and told her good luck with her life and her bastard children. He ended the call by advising Mini that he would always be there when she was ready to come back to the streets, but until then, not to contact him. It broke her heart and she cried for hours and Luther was right there holding her. She eventually let it go, and did what she had to do for her children.

Hoover was street raised. He was a pimp and had been her pimp as well as her pusher. Hoover was the reason she had been a prostitute and a junkie. Even after her kids, he still had her in the streets, letting her get clean long enough to ensure her children weren't born addicts, and then the second they were born, he doped her up again and put her back on the streets. Mini had welcomed the high. She needed it to get her through the hundreds of men she was sleeping with, doing unthinkable things with. But she eventually had enough.

It took her daughter looking at her one night and asking if she would be like her when she grew up to be her wake up call. Mini had to change her life. Otherwise, her daughter would indeed have grown up to be just like her. Hoover would have made sure of it.

So from that day on, she was mother and father to her children, until Luther walked into her life. And now, after all those years of him waiting, she was finally ready. He had promised to wait, and that he did, so the least she could do was be for him what he had been for her all these years.

"I know, and I will. It's just hard, you know?" She offered a kiss before resting her head on his shoulder.

*****

Logic sat across from Joy at Intrigued, admiring her beauty as she listened to a local artist perform on stage. She seemed so into the song that she hadn't even noticed that he was watching her. Things had been so out of control with everything going on that Logic just needed a minute to step back. He had missed Joy, and as patient as she was being, he knew that she had missed him too. Logic loved that she didn't complain. She accepted everything he told her, and never once made him feel bad about the late nights and hours that he left her alone. She had proven to be someone he could rely on, and a woman who would support him without question. He loved that about her. Hell, he loved everything about her because he simply loved Joy.

"I feel you watching me." Joy grinned, but kept her eyes on the stage.

Logic smiled at her confession.

"You're beautiful. I like what I see," he said as he lifted his hand and let his fingers glide across her neck.

They weren't side by side, but they were close. He needed her to be within reach so when the urge hit to touch her, he could.

"You always say that, but you have to." Joys eyes were on him this time as she leaned over slightly to sip from her straw without lifting her glass.

Her statement made him smile again. "I don't have to say anything. I say it because it's true."

She looked him right in the eyes, lips in a thin line, and eyes not giving away her mood. "You have to because I'm yours."

Logic grabbed the seat of Joy's chair and moved it closer to him so that their legs were touching and his hand was holding onto her chin. "You are mine, but that doesn't mean I have to say you're beautiful. I say it because you are."

Logic kissed Joy with several light pecks before he slid is tongue into her mouth and gave her his all. He was addicted to the way her lips felt and tasted. After their kiss, Joy blushed and looked around. She caught Felicia watching the two of them and the way her face transformed into a frown caused Joy's smile to quickly fade. Felicia was jealous, which made Joy wonder if she still had reason to be.

"She's not happy," Joy said, leaning back in her chair as she began to play with the fries on the plate of food in front of her. They were what was left of the meal that she and Logic had shared, since neither of them were really hungry.

Knowing that there were potentially a lot of "shes" in Intrigued that Joy could be referring to, he turned his head slightly to see who she was talking about. When his eyes met with Felicia's and he noticed the hatred that radiated from them, he chuckled and kissed Joy again.

"Her happiness is no concern of mine. She's not you," was his only explanation.

"Does she have a reason to be?"

"A reason to be what? Unhappy?"

"Yeah, about you and me."

Logic looked at Joy and then lifted his beer. He turned it up and then set it on the table. "Of course she does, she wants what you have," he said arrogantly, but only because he was stating the truth.

Joy searched his face, trying to find meaning in his words before she released her next question. "When was the last time you were with her? I know you've been with her. I can tell."

He chuckled. Women always had things figured out, who you slept with and why. He thought it was cute that Joy was jealous, but she had nothing to worry about. "The first night we hung out."

Joy's head popped up from her drink and she looked at him in disbelief. "You had sex with her and then hung out with me?"

"No, I hung out with you and then had sex with her. We weren't together, Joy. What difference does that make? Especially now. I damn sure ain't with her now, and don't want to be."

She thought about it for a minute. It mattered to her, but he was right, they weren't together back then, so there wasn't really anything that she could say about it. But it still bothered her. Maybe that was why Felicia was so upset. Maybe there had been other times after that.

She stared at him while the thought flowed through her head, but she didn't want an argument, so she left it alone.

Logic stood, leaned over the back of her chair before nuzzling his face in her neck. He kissed it several times before he forced her head back enough to reach her lips.

"I know your mind is doing summersaults. That was the last time I've been with anyone except you, so let it go. I'm all yours, and that's not going to change. I need to go holler at Luther real quick. I'll be right back."

He was still holding the sides of her face while her head tilted back against his stomach, so he kissed her one last time. After he smiled at her and released her face, Logic made his way to the back where Luther's office was.

Logic walked into Luther's office, causing him to look up. He sat across from Luther's desk and leaned back.

"Did you find out anything?" he tossed out casually.

Luther pulled the glasses he was wearing from his face and held them in his hand as he leaned back and rocked slowly in his oversized leather chair. His eyes were on Logic as he mentally prepared to tell him what he knew.

"Is it that bad?" Logic chuckled. He knew Luther well enough to know his mannerisms, and could tell he was stalling.

"The person locked up was Rah Tremble. I'm sure you already knew that, which was why you asked," Luther began.

"Yeah, I figured. How long he in there for?" Logic was glad that Rah couldn't get to his family, especially Joy, but he still didn't want him in jail, he wanted him dead.

"He's out, his lawyer called in some really big favors. Because with his record and what they caught him with, there shouldn't have been any way for her to get him out, but she did it. She got him out a few hours after they locked him up."

"Fuck," he mumbled under his breath. That put him right back at square one. He knew he had to find Rah before Rah found him.

"I'm not going to ask what you have going on, but there's something else you need to know."

"What's that?"

Luther looked Logic right in the eyes. "Joy's last name is Malone, right?"

Logic remembered having a conversation with Luther about Joy's parents. Shortly after, Luther looked into them both, even though he never discussed it with Logic.

"Yeah, why?"

"Marilyn Malone was the lawyer he called. That's who got him out."

Logic shook his head in disbelief. "You have got to be fucking kidding me."

"Don't do anything you can't take back," Luther said, referring to Marilyn.

Logic understood that to mean that Luther was warning him about who Marilyn was. Not only was she a lawyer who apparently had a lot of connections, but when it was all said and done, she was still Joy's mother.

"I'm good on that. I appreciate it."

Logic stood to leave, and Luther retuned his glasses to his face before looking up at him. "Go see your mother soon. You know she's worried about you and needs to see your face."

"I just saw her this morning at your crib, or did you forget?" Logic pointed at Luther with a slight grin. He wasn't thrilled about having a front row seat to his mother's personal life, but he was glad it was Luther.

Luther looked down at his computer and laughed before he roughly began pounding the keys. "You know what I mean. Just check in with her."

"I got you."

With that, Logic left Luther's office plotting his next move.

# -6-

Logic kept his eyes on Joy while she waited patiently for him to explain why he didn't want her out right now. It didn't have a damn thing to do with her being in a club without him, but everything to do with the fact that her mother had gotten Rah out of jail, and Logic didn't have a clue how to find him.

"I just don't think it's a good idea," Logic said calmly, in anticipation of how he assumed Joy was going to react. It would do no good for both of them to be erratic right now, so he chose to remain calm.

"I'm going to be with Karma, your sister, and your cousin. I know you don't possibly think that I would do anything stupid."

A smirk spread across his face, which forced a frown on Joy's. Logic was amused by the fact that she assumed he was worried about her with another man.

"Nah, that shit ain't cross my mind because I know you know better. Besides, I would solve that problem by sliding up in your shit before I let you go. My issue is that Rah is out there on some bullshit. If he puts his hands on you, Najah, or Nova, I might end up in jail because I'm going kill his ass and I won't give a fuck who's around to see it."

Joy sat there trying to figure out which statement to address first. She was floored by both of them, but she knew Logic, and she knew that he meant every word without a shadow of doubt.

"Rah is not stupid enough to come after either one of us, knowing that you're after him. Besides, we'll be in a club full of people. There's nothing he can do without someone seeing him. I'll be fine, we'll be fine."

Again, Logic was quiet while he processed. Everything in him was yelling no, but he understood her need for some type of normalcy in her life. Since they had been together, her life had conformed to functioning around just him. A lot of it had to do with the fact that the whole Rah situation had Logic holding on tight, but that was on him, not on her.

Joy was sitting across the room from where Logic stood. He was leaning against the wall in the living room while she sat on the sofa studying his body language and waiting for his reaction.

After a few minutes of silence, she decided to resort to Plan B. Joy knew that Logic was weak under her touch, so she stood and walked over to him. His eyes were on her the entire time, but his expression didn't change. Even after her hand grasped his belt buckle and she leveraged her body against his, his expression remained unreadable. She used her free hand to slide around his neck until her arm was roped around it. Their eyes were still connected, and he hadn't moved. His arms were still at his sides while her body was pressed against his.

"I just want one night to hang out with my girls and not think about all the other stuff." Joy lifted her weight onto her toes and kissed his chin first, then his jaw line, and last she planted her lips onto his.

Logic finally released a smile. His hands moved up the back of Joy's legs until they rested on her butt.

"You ain't slick, Joy."

"What?" She looked up at him and bit her bottom lip so that her smile wouldn't show.

They both knew that she was trying to sway his decision by being close to him.

"You know what, and don't think I can't say no because you rubbing all up on my body." Logic leaned down and kissed Joy again before he tilted his head slightly to the side and stared at her.

He knew that if she didn't go to the club that she would be home alone anyway. Gotti had called with word that their people had located Moses, which meant that he would be handled tonight. He had been with Alicia since he was released from the hospital. Logic knew that if anything happened, there was a chance that he wouldn't be able to get to her since he and Gotti planned to go after Moses. That was his biggest hesitation.

Joy laughed. I'm not trying to sway your decision. Maybe I just wanted to be close to you," she insisted and then tucked her lip under her teeth again because it was a lie and she knew it.

"Yeah, whatever. You can go, but I need you to check in." He pecked her lips. "A lot."

"Done." Joy grinned before kissing him again and then tried to pull away, but he held her in place.

"Nah, we got something to take care of first." His grin now matched hers.

"I need to text your sister back and call Karma."

"Nah, you need to come up out of these so I can slide up in you real quick. I wasn't playing."

Logic worked his hands into her leggings and pushed them down over her hips. He damn sure wasn't playing, and he hoped Joy knew that. He was about to be so deep in her that she would feel it every time she moved tonight. Logic wasn't a jealous man, but he wasn't stupid either. He knew what he had in Joy, and he wanted her to be very clear about what she had in him, so he was about to make sure her body had a constant reminder.

*****

"So, he still there?" Were the first words out of Logic's mouth when he met Gotti on the block.

"Yeah, he's in there. Hasn't been out since he left the hospital. Word is he's hiding from his brother. Rah's been out for a minute, and everybody knows that Moses sent the cops there, which is how he got knocked." Lil Chris spoke up first since it was him and Roger who had found Moses.

Gotti and Logic eyed each other for a brief moment since the two of them were the only ones who knew all the details of what was going on. Lil Chris' girl had just had a baby, so he hadn't really been around much, and even if he had, Logic felt like the fewer people involved the better. It wasn't that he didn't trust his team, because he did, whole heartedly, but he also felt it was best that he and Gotti handle the situation on their own. Gotti agreed, so their team had very little detail about the situation.

"Aight, bet. We're heading out. You got shit covered around here?" Logic asked.

"Yeah, I'm good. We busy as fuck, though," Lil Chris said with a smirk before he emptied the backpack he was carrying.

Rolls of cash hit the table and Logic smiled. Money was good right now. All of the traffic flow from Rah and Moses' area was coming their way since neither Rah or Moses was currently focused on the block.

"That's what the fuck I'm talking about." Gotti lifted a few of the bands and then placed them back on the table.

"Yo, make sure someone keeps an eye on the house. Get this counted and in the safe as soon as possible. We're not used to keeping this much cash around here, and niggas be on some bullshit. Last thing we need is someone running up in here," Gotti said, sharing a quick glance with Logic first, who nodded in approval.

"Word. I got it covered. I'm 'bout to count this right now and Rog is out front. So we should be good."

Gotti and Logic both nodded, dapped Lil' Chris before they left out and locked up. Not long after, they were in Logic's car and heading to the location that Lil Chris had given them for Moses.

"No word on Rah yet?"

"Nah, not yet, but I have a few things I plan on checking into." Logic had an idea that it was possible for Rah to be hiding out at Joy's parents' house. If Rah wasn't actually there, then Marilyn was going to tell him exactly where he was, and Logic planned to use any means necessary to get the information from her.

"You wanna tell me what that is?" Gotti glanced at Logic but then directed his focus back to his phone.

"Not yet." Being that it was Joy's mother, Logic felt like he needed to handle the situation alone. He didn't really want witnesses if things didn't go as planned.

Gotti nodded. He never questioned Logic's moves. He didn't have to, they just had an understanding about certain things.

"Yo, they just hit the club," Gotti announced after reading a text he received from Najah.

Logic was about to respond to Gotti but his phone went off with a notification too. He glanced at the screen while it sat in his cup holder. When he realized it was Joy, a smile crept across his face. He could only imagine what it said. She wasn't very happy with him when she left to meet Karma, thanks to the punishing he had put on her body. Logic had made Joy cum so many times that he had her rethinking her decision to go out in the first place. He made sure there was no question about his ability to please her, and it was evident from the way she was struggling after their session.

He'd offered to kiss it and make it better, but she wouldn't let him anywhere near her after she found the energy to make it into the shower. He smiled even harder when he thought about the fact that he had to steal a kiss before she left because she was dead serious about keeping her distance from him.

"Hopefully we'll be done with this shit soon, and then we can head there."

"Yo, we doing a ride through our we shutting that shit down?" Gotti asked.

He had every intention of pulling Najah up out the club and taking her home with him. He was still standing firm on no sex, but he had his mind on a few other things they could do. On top of that, he didn't want some other nigga in her face pushing up on her. She was already his, he just had to sit on it for a minute so that he could get his personal life situated.

Gotti wasn't committed to anyone, but there were a few out there who were damn sure committed to him. He didn't want Najah to have to deal with that, so out of respect for her, he was going to handle a few things before he made shit official with him and Najah

"You do whatever the fuck you need to do, but I'm taking Joy's ass home. Girls night is over after we handle this shit with Moses."

Gotti laughed at how serious Logic was. At least they were on the same page with that.

It took them about twenty minutes to get to Alicia's apartment. It was a complex with three levels, but lucky for them, she had a first floor apartment. Gotti and Logic both strapped up, pulled on latex gloves, and got out. It was almost eleven, so the parking lot was empty. They hid their guns on their bodies, but kept their hands on them.

When they reached the apartment door, Gotti and Logic both had guns in hand.

"How the fuck we supposed to get in that bitch without setting him off?" Gotti asked.

Neither of them had figured out the small yet important details. In fact, the only thing that either of them had on their minds was taking Moses's life.

Logic looked at the door and shrugged. "Shit, one of us can shoot the lock off and the other can aim at whatever's coming our way. We just better not fucking miss. I damn sure ain't in the mood to catch a hot one tonight."

Gotti looked at him and laughed. "I got the fucking lock. Your ass can aim."

Gotti aimed his gun at the lock, and just before he was about to fire off a shot, they heard the lock turn and then Moses appeared. Logic's gun hit him right in the forehead, pressing hard into his skull as Moses backed up and lifted his hands. He gritted his teeth and flinched due his injuries, from where Logic had previously shot him in the shoulder.

"Well, well, look what the fuck we have here." Logic took a step toward Moses, forcing him back.

"Man, fuck both of you. Shit, I ain't worried."

"Bruh, you should be, but fuck it. If your ass has been sipping on courage tonight, then we're cool with that too.

"I ain't scared to die. Do what the fuck you gotta do."

Just as Moses finished his sentence they heard a pop and a bullet hit the door. Gotti looked up just in time to catch Alicia before she fired off another shot.

"Damn, can't your ass do anything right? Your dumb ass almost hit me," Moses yelled.

Gotti realized that Alicia was shaky and afraid. She had no clue about shooting a gun, and if he had to guess, Moses had tossed it to her right before he left and told her to defend herself.

"Yo, you have a daughter. This nigga here is about to die. Don't make her grow up without a mother too. Put that shit down." Logic had both his eyes and gun on Moses, so he didn't even bother to look at Alicia as he spoke to her.

"I can shoot your ass before you even think about pulling that trigger again, and trust me, I won't miss. Put that shit on the floor and kick it out the way." Gotti nodded at the gun Alicia was holding.

She looked across at Moses, Logic, and then Gotti before she slowly kneeled to the floor. Once she placed the gun in front of her, she stood and lifted her hands in the air in a gesture indicating surrender.

Gotti pushed past Moses and Logic. When he reached Alicia, he forcefully grabbed her arm and shoved her down onto the sofa before he picked up the gun and dropped the clip out of it. He cleared the chamber and placed the clip and bullets in his pocket before tossing the gun on the sofa next to her.

"That's about all you need. You know your ass don't know a damn thing about shooting a fucking gun. You're about to let his dumb ass cost you your life." Gotti looked down at her, wearing an irritated expression.

Both Logic and Gotti were now in the apartment with the door shut.

"Damn, yo, we don't even know each other and you sent your peoples to take my life. The fuck I do to you?" Logic wore a smirk which grew wider as the scowl on Moses face intensified.

"Nigga, we not 'bout to have a conversation. Like I said, I ain't afraid to die, so do that shit if that's what you here to do." He damn near growled through gritted teeth.

Logic chuckled, amused by how hard Moses was pretending to be. He knew Moses was afraid; he could see it in his eyes. No matter how tough they were, no man facing a losing battle with death was without some type of fear. Even if it was just a little.

"I came all this way just to see you and this snitching ass bitch, and you can't even give me a conversation? That's some foul shit, Moses."

Logic calling Alicia a snitch quickly got her attention. He could see her from the corner of his eyes and could tell the moment she finally realized that they knew her role in what had happened at First and Prospect.

"Yeah, bitch, I know you're the one who sent the cops there. No need for you to be sitting there looking all fucking stupid now." Logic's voice traveled across the room and sent chills through Alicia.

"Yous a dumb ass bitch." Moses snarled as his eyes moved across the room to where she was sitting. His voice caused her to jump a little. "Your dumb ass sent the damn cops there? The fuck were you thinking? You got everybody in the streets thinking I'm a fucking snitch. If you had just done what I asked, this nigga would be dead and we wouldn't be here. I swear Imma fuck you up." Moses was so pissed he actually tried to pull away from Logic just to get to Alicia, but reality quickly set in again when he felt the barrel of Logic's gun press firmly against his forehead.

"Damn, Logic, he mad as fuck," Gotti said before he laughed.

"You didn't know? She didn't tell you? See, the father of her child meant more to her than you. She didn't want him to die. I guess I can understand that shit. I mean, family is important, right?" Logic knew that mentioning his brother and Alicia's child would strike a nerve.

"I swear on everything, your ass is dead too. If he don't kill you, I'll damn sure find a way to make that shit happen." Moses pointed to Alicia who finally released the tears that where building in her eyes.

"Man, chill. That shit is old news. I'm alive, you're about to die, your brother's gonna die." Logic shrugged. "Don't sweat that shit."

"Just do it then, damn. The fuck you bitchin' up for?"

"That nigga just called you a bitch, Logic. The fuck?" Gotti laughed.

Logic chuckled. "I know. That shit hurt my feelings too, damn."

"You're dumb as fuck, yo. Just shoot that nigga so we can go."

Logic looked right at Moses. "Aight." He pulled the trigger.

Moses hit the floor and Alicia screamed.

"Shut the fuck up, damn." Gotti yelled, narrowing his eyes at her.

Logic walked over and looked at Alicia. He didn't have the heart to take her life. He saw his sister when he looked at her.

"You fucked me once, that shit won't happen again. Dealing with niggas like Moses and Rah will cause you and your daughter to lose your lives. Do you want that? Do you want to put your daughter's life in jeopardy like that?"

She wiped her tears and quickly shook her head no. "Just let me go. I won't tell anybody, I swear."

"Man fuck that. Her ass got five-oh on speed dial," Gotti said, mugging her hard as hell. He also had a soft spot being that she was a mother, but he too wanted to scare her.

"I don't, I swear I don't. I'm leaving anyway. I'm taking my daughter and heading to New York to live with my aunt. You won't see or hear from me again. Please, just let me go." She was crying hysterically now, with tears and snot everywhere.

She snorted, and was damn near hyperventilating. Raising a shaky hand, she pointed to the corner where two suitcases were sitting, as well as what looked like an overstuffed baby bag and a car seat.

Gotti and Logic shared a glance after surveying the luggage.

"Look, you get one chance, but fuck around if you want to, and you end up like that." Logic pointed to Moses' lifeless body on the floor.

"I won't, I'm leaving, tonight. I promise. I was heading to the airport after he left. He didn't know, he thought I was leaving with him, but I wasn't. I can't keep doing this. I can show you."

She looked back and forth between the two, as if requesting permission to move. Logic nodded and she stood slowly and made her way to the counter where there was an oversized purse. She pulled out what appeared to be a plane ticket and extended it to Logic. He glanced at it, noticing it was indeed a one-way flight to New York, so he nodded a second time.

"Aight, you get a pass, but make a call before you leave and I'll find your ass. Trust me. I have people everywhere," Logic lied.

He'd left New York as a kid, and the only person he knew there was his father, and he wouldn't contact his bitch ass for anything. But she didn't know that.

"I won't, I promise."

"Yo, what about Rah? You heard from that nigga?" Gotti asked.

Alicia thought about lying, but considered Logic's words. If he would kill her for calling the cops, he would surely kill her for withholding information.

"Some woman got him out. She put him up in a hotel downtown. He called Moses and they talked, but then Moses hung up and said that he had to find his brother before Rah found him. He said that Rah was just fronting and that he knew Moses had set him up. I didn't tell him that I was the one who called the cops, so he thought that Rah just knew that Moses had sent someone there to kill him."

"What hotel?"

"I don't know. I just know its downtown and nice. The lady is rich. He's even driving one of her cars. A black Range Rover."

"When was this?" Logic asked, now even more pissed that Marilyn's dumb ass was hiding Rah, and too stupid to understand what that meant for Joy's safety

"A little while ago. That's why Moses was leaving. He said he had to handle Rah, and then we were leaving here, but I couldn't. I had to think about my daughter, so I lied to him and told him I was. My aunt had already bought me a ticket to come to New York. Moses just didn't know that."

"Last chance, and I mean that. You fuck this up and your daughter grows up an orphan. Don't fuck me or I promise you'll regret it," Logic said in a way that resonated with Alicia.

She nodded and agreed. Her life was far too important to lose for Moses or Rah.

"Yo, let's roll." Logic walked toward the door and Gotti followed.

At this point, Logic was on a mission to find Rah, and he was starting with Marilyn. But right now he needed to get Joy out of that club. With Rah on the loose, he didn't feel comfortable with her being out in a club without him there to make sure she was good.

"Damn, it's crowded in here. This the exact reason why I don't do clubs." Nova scrunched up her face and looked around.

They four of them were seated in one of the lounge areas. Karma and Joy were on one sofa while Najah and Nova were across from them on another. The DJ had been doing his thing, so this was the first time they had been seated since they got there. They were now scoping out potential candidates for Nova to kick it to since she was the only unattached one in the crew.

"Aye, boo. He's cute, what about him?" Najah pointed across the half wall that separated them from the walkway leading to the railing that overlooked the lower level of the club. They all had eyes on a really cute guy whom they assumed Najah was referencing. He wasn't super tall, roughly six feet, but he had a handsome face and nice build.

Nova looked at her cousin before she followed the direction that Najah was pointing and rolled her eyes. "Girl, bye. He's that body builder type. You know what that means." Nova sucked her teeth and rolled her eyes again.

"What?" Karma asked.

"He ain't working with nothing. The more they pump them muscles up, the smaller it gets. Hell, most of them don't have nothing to start with in the first place, and that's why they walk around looking like they on steroids."

Karma, Joy and Najah looked at each other and laughed. "Damn, boo, you speaking from the heart over there. Who disappointed you?" Karma was looking right at Nova.

Joy glanced at the crew, just glad that they were all getting along now. When they first got there, it was tense because Karma could hold a grudge for days, and she was still pissed about how things went down at Mini's house the night Rah showed up and showed out. She wasn't even there, but Joy had told her about it. Joy was her girl, so she was going to defend her to the end no matter who was coming for her, even Logic's sister and cousin.

Thankfully, after a few drinks and a little conversation, Karma had realized they were all over it and cool with Joy. She had let it go, but reserved the right to beat ass if either of them got wrong again. Karma was just like that.

"Girl, he ain't even worth talking about, but trust me, it's true. Overdo it on muscle, under do it on the package," Nova said, causing them all to smile.

"What about me? What am I working with?"

A very nice chocolate dream stepped around the half wall from the section behind them and stood right in front of Nova. His stare made her uncomfortable because it was so intense.

"Damn. You got to be working with something nice, cause you too damn fine to be a disappointment," Karma said, causing Joy to punch her in the arm.

"What? I ain't blind and neither are you."

He chuckled about Karma's statement but kept his eyes on Nova. "I'm waiting."

She eyed his body, gauging his features. Chocolate skin, low cut Cesar, full sexy lips, and athletic build. His body was nice, but not overdone.

"Man, I'm not about to discuss your body up in here in front of all these people," Nova said. She had already checked for a print, but his jeans were hiding whatever he was working with.

"So you can play dude out, but you don't want to give me your honest opinion? And those are you girls, right? You've been chilling with them all night, so I'm sure they won't mind."

"Nope, Nova, tell him. We don't mind," Joy said with a grin.

"Nope, not at all. In fact, I would love to hear your opinion about what chocolate dream here is working with," Najah said.

After being put on the spot, Nova froze and snapped on Joy and Najah. "How about the two of you mind your business, Logic and Gotti?" Nova made a point of calling them by their men's names, which made Joy smirk and Najah laugh.

"Yo, it's cool. How about this?" Dude reached in his pocket and pulled out his phone. "My boy is ready to jet anyway, so you give me your number and we can have a private conversation about it later. That work for you? I really want to hear your opinion."

"Yeah, Nova, he really wants to hear your opinion on what his dick game is like," Karma said and giggled.

"I'm about to slap every single one of you," Nova said and rolled her eyes.

Dude laughed and then looked at Nova with that damn death stare again. "So, do we have a deal? Or are you gonna make my home boy clown me for the rest of the night? He's watching, so if you don't give me your number, I'll never hear the end of it. You wouldn't do me like that, would you?"

He offered up the sexiest grin and Nova melted. She reached for his phone, entered her number, and then handed it back to him. After he looked down at her entry, his eyes were on her again.

"Nova, I like that. I could get used to saying that." She blushed. "This is your real number, right? You wouldn't play me out, would you?"

"It's real," she said.

"Aight, well I'll hit you later. You beautiful ladies enjoy the rest of your night."

After he was gone, the ladies wasted no time at all offering up their opinions on what had just happened, beginning with Najah.

"Girl, why the hell didn't you leave with his sexy ass? He clearly wanted you to evaluate his situation." Najah had her finger pointed at her cousin with a curious grin on her face.

"Yassss, boo. You should have been like, 'that will take some hands on evaluating, which I will be more than happy to commit to'," Karma said.

"Girl, yes, that evaluation would have been just for fun. Anybody that damn cocky has got be working with something serious," Joy added.

"You would know, wouldn't you?" Karma looked across her shoulder at Joy and grinned. "Don't think I haven't noticed that your ass can barely walk tonight. You're struggling, boo, and your man is king of cocky, and apparently the king of cock too."

"I'm fine, and you need to mind your business." Joy adjusted her body so that she could sit a little more comfortably.

Najah laughed. "Nah, boo, she's right. My brother put that 'your ass better not even look at another man tonight' hurting on you before he let you out. Auggie ain't slick. He knew what he was doing."

Nova frowned. "Can we please not go there? That's just nasty, that's my damn cousin."

Joy rolled her eyes and Najah laughed.

"Joy, you know her? She damn sure all in your grill like she wanna say something." Najah pointed to the left of where they were sitting and everyone's eyes followed.

Sure enough, Felicia was with some other chick who was clearly a chick, but looked and dressed like a dude. Both of them had their eyes on Joy. They didn't bother to pretend that they weren't staring either when Joy and her crew looked their way.

"No, but your brother does," Joy announced, feeling annoyed that Felicia was there and staring her down.

Nova and Najah looked at each other and then right back at Joy. "Knows her how? That's my brother and everything, but if he's on some fuck shit, we can handle that," Najah said and she meant it. She had grown to like Joy even after they had a slight rift, so if Logic called himself being on some disrespectful type stuff then she was going to check him and whoever this hoe was that was staring them down.

"I guess they had something before us." Joy shrugged, not really concerned about Felicia. Logic had already made it clear that there was nothing there and she believed him, but this chick was seriously trying her patience.

"So the bitch still living in the past. She better get her damn eyes in check before I become a part of her future," Najah said.

"Yeah, her and that trick she's with, looking like she's in need of a damn shape up with her baldheaded ass." Karma rolled her eyes.

All four ladies burst out laughing as they looked right at their spectators.

Them laughing and joking didn't sit well with Felicia because she knew from the way they all turned and faced her that they were talking about her. It was bad enough that Joy had Logic, and sitting there watching her gloat about it wasn't helping the situation.

"Oh shit, this hoe is crazy. She is seriously about to come over here so I can check her ass," Najah said, standing to her feet.

Nova and Karma followed, but Joy stayed put because she wanted to see if Felicia would actually address her.

As soon as they were close enough, Najah asked, "Can we help you?" before Felicia had a chance to open her mouth.

"No, but apparently I can help you since you all in my damn face," Felicia said.

Joy looked right at her and laughed.

"Bitch please, you the one with the eye problem. You need some help with that?" Karma said.

"Fe, don't sweat these hoes, especially that one. She won't have him for long, you know like I know. If you want him, you can have him. Anytime. Let's roll." The chick that was with Felicia said with smirk looking right a Joy, who looked up with a grin, not moved by any of what was going on.

"You need to listen to your boyfriend and keep it moving," Joy said in reference to the fact that Felicia's friend actually looked like a dude with her low cut hair, ashy skin, t-shirt and baggy cargo shorts that hung low around her waist.

"Bitch, you talking mighty slick, but you ain't moving," Felicia's friend snapped.

Joy finally stood and stepped past Karma, who was standing slightly in front of Najah and Nova.

"Do you really want to wear an ass whooping because your girl is all in her feelings about a man who has clearly moved on? I mean, it doesn't matter to me either." A cocky grin spread across Karma's face as she squared up, ready for one of them to make a move.

"Cori, let's go. Fuck them." Felicia grabbed her friend's arm.

Although she knew that Cori had hands, she didn't, and the four of them looked like they were ready to use theirs. She had underestimated how Joy would react.

"This hoe's name is Cori. Fucking priceless. No wonder she looks like a dude," Najah said and laughed so hard it pissed Cori off.

She swung on Najah, but somebody caught her arm before she made contact.

"Nah, shorty, it's not going down like that," Gotti said from behind her, causing Cori to turn and almost swing on him until she realized it was a guy.

"The fuck going on here?" Logic asked as he stepped between Karma and Joy. Once he was behind Joy, his arm moved around her waist until their bodies were close.

Felicia looked like she wanted to cry.

"This hoe seems confused about past and present," Nova said, pointing to Felicia.

"Man, get the fuck out of here with that bullshit. She knows it ain't noting. Now try to act like you don't." He gave Felicia a look that made her regret that she had even stepped to them in the first place.

"If it ain't nothing, then you need to tell this hoe to—"

Before she could finish her sentence, Joy popped her right in the mouth. "Bitch, my name is Joy. If you gonna talk about me, the least you can do is get my damn name right."

Felicia grabbed her mouth as tears filled her eyes. She just looked at Joy, knowing that she couldn't defend herself.

Cori was next to her yelling all types of bitches before she waved her hand at Felicia, irritated that she had stepped up to defend her and she wouldn't even defend her damn self. She walked off cussing and mumbling, not really caring what happened to Felicia at that point.

Logic laughed. "Yo, let's go. This is exactly why I didn't want you up in here, because of stupid shit like this. In here acting like a fucking hood rat over some irrelevant bitch."

Logic's eyes went right to Felicia before he grabbed Joy's hand and shook his head as he walked past her. He stopped just outside the area they had been sitting in when he realized that Nova and Najah were still standing there.

"The fuck you waiting for? I said, let's go," he roared.

Najah was the first to move because she could feel Gotti's eyes on her, and he looked as annoyed as Logic did. When she made it to the entrance of their area, he grabbed her arm and pulled her toward him.

"How did you get here?" He looked down at Najah and she couldn't really read his expression as his eyes moved up and down her body and then stopped at her face.

"Nova," Najah said.

"Your son good for the night, or we need to go get him?"

Najah cocked her head to the side and looked at him curiously. Her mother had Trent, so he would be good for the night. "No, he's with my mom."

"Aight, bet, you're going with me." He walked away without saying anything else.

Najah didn't know what else to do, so she followed.

The six of them made their way through the club and none of them stopped until they were out front. Karma and Joy said their goodbyes. Karma left and Joy sat in Logic's car while she waited for him to address Najah and Nova. When he was done and in the car with her, he leaned back so that his body was slightly against his door and he was facing Joy as he stared at her.

"What?" Joy asked when he didn't say anything.

"That shit in there ain't even you, Joy. The fuck is that about? Didn't I tell you that there wasn't shit there and that I don't want that damn girl? Yet, you got your ass in there arguing with her like you don't have no damn sense. Forget that hoe," he yelled, pointing toward the club.

Joy laughed sarcastically. "I wasn't arguing with her about you. And I popped her ass in the mouth because she was being disrespectful. That wasn't about you. Why are you mad? She must matter."

"Man, don't even... How the fuck you fix your face to say some bullshit like that? If I want her I can have her, and any other female out there if we're being honest. You know that shit too, but I'm with you. I'm not gonna be with somebody who can't believe that enough to let bullshit like that go. Why the fuck you gonna entertain somebody who's fronting you about shit that you own? That makes your ass look dumb and insecure. You should have just ignored her dumb ass and kept it moving."

Logic started his car and pulled out of the parking lot. He was annoyed. He had enough other shit to worry about, and Joy showing her ass in a club over Felicia wasn't something he needed right now.

Joy didn't even respond. She wasn't about to argue with him about the fact that he couldn't keep his past hoes in check. The drive to his house was quiet. They were both so stubborn that neither of them broke. Even after they reached his apartment, Logic and Joy both stayed quiet. She was pissed that he was upset about his past starting shit with her, and he was pissed that Joy had even entertained it.

The two of them walked around his apartment like the other didn't exist, which was hard to do because the space was so small. But with everything in them, they were both trying. This went on for a while, Logic in the living room while Joy was in the bedroom. They both had managed to shower, change and go to their separate corners without saying one word to each other, but it was killing them both.

Logic was suffering the most because after dealing with Moses, he needed Joy to settle his mind. Her body next to his, wrapped around him, erased all things in his life that he didn't want to think about, even if it was temporary. And he wanted that right now.

"Fuck it," he mumbled to himself before he stood from where he was sitting on the sofa.

He laughed and shook his head, knowing that Joy had a hold on him. He loved it, but at the same time hated it because he was powerless against her. His free will was gone because she controlled it.

The second he rounded the corner to the hallway his body collided with Joy's which made him grin. He grabbed her arms to stop her from stumbling back from the force of their contact.

"You looking for me?" Logic asked, still holding onto Joy's arms.

"Depends, were you looking for me?"

"Maybe."

"This is weird, it feels weird," Joy admitted. She had been struggling with the idea of them being there together but not talking. They didn't argue much and when they did, it never lasted long.

"Then stop being mad at me and let me come lay down with you."

Logic released Joy's arms and grabbed her around the waist, pulling her body into his. He lowered his head so that their foreheads pressed gently together and just stared into her eyes.

"I'm not mad at you, and it's your apartment. I can't tell you where to go in it."

"I need you right now, fuck all that other shit. It's not important, so can we be over this?"

Joy smiled softly at the fact that he needed her. "Yes."

Logic looked down at Joy and slowly moved his hand up her back to her neck. He gently gripped it before his lips connected with hers.

"Look, I don't give a fuck who gets in your face or has a confession about something they think they have with me. It's all bullshit. This right here is the truth, so don't let anyone make you think any different. You got me, Joy. I promise you that. There's not a chance in hell that anyone else can touch that. So don't be out there on that bullshit showing your ass because some hoe is in her feelings about me. I don't give a fuck, and you shouldn't either. We good on that?"

"Yeah."

"Now can we go lay down so that I can slide up in this?"

Logic grinned as his hand moved between Joy's legs, but she caught his wrist.

"We can go lay down so that we can go to sleep. You're on a temporary hold after earlier, and you know why."

Logic kissed Joy on the neck and then laughed, "Yeah, aight, but trust me, that shit better be temporary. You can't be holding out on me."

Joy rolled her eyes as he took her hand and the two made their way to his bedroom. She was still sore from earlier and not about to even consider making that worse. After the two got comfortable, Logic made sure Joy's body was wrapped around his, with his face nuzzled in her neck. Just that quickly he was at peace. The fruity scent that clung to her skin, and the rhythm of her heartbeat were like heaven to him, and exactly what he needed. It didn't take long for the two to be out.

# -8-

Najah had been sitting alone in Gotti's bedroom since they got in from the club. He hadn't really said much to her the entire drive to his house, and when they got there, it was the same. Aside from him getting her stuff to shower with and one of his t-shirts to wear when she was done, they hadn't really been near each other. He was in the living room on the phone while she was in his room. She could tell from the conversation that it was business, but she was still annoyed that he was ignoring her. Why the hell did he want her to come home with him if all he was going to do was talk on the phone and ignore her all night?

If he was upset about the whole club thing, then he didn't have a right to be. She wasn't his girl, which meant that he didn't have a right to be upset about her behavior. Even knowing that, it was driving her crazy that he was ignoring her, so after fighting it as long as she could, she crawled off his bed and went to find him.

When she entered his living room, she found him on the sofa, leaned back with one arm folded above his head while he rolled sections of his short spike dreads between his fingers. His chest was bare, exposing tattoo covered muscles that flexed with the movement of his arm above his head. His other hand was deep inside the sweatpants he wore while he held his phone in place with his shoulder.

She walked over to him and stopped a few feet away, arms folded and just stared at him. It took him a minute to acknowledge her presence, which he did on purpose.

"Yo, Chevy, let me hit you back," Gotti said while his eyes roamed Najah's body.

He kept his expression neutral, but he wanted to smile at the way his oversized shirt swallowed her small frame. He also knew that there was nothing under it because the boxers he offered her wouldn't stay up around her waist no matter how many times she rolled the waist band.

Once he finished the call, he dropped his phone in his lap. He didn't bother to remove the hand that was in his sweatpants because his erection was growing, and he was trying to keep it under control.

"I think I'm just going to head home. I mean, it seems like you're busy."

Gotti didn't say anything while his eyes continued to roam her body, which had Najah feeling uncomfortable. She began to fidget with the hem of his shirt, while she adjusted her weight from foot to foot.

"You wanna leave?" he asked when he finally spoke up.

"If you're going to keep ignoring me, then yeah," Najah said with a massive attitude.

Gotti chuckled and removed his hand from his sweatpants. Najah's eyes followed his movement and damn near popped out her head when she noticed the imprint that he had left exposed.

"Come here," he commanded.

She frowned a little before she moved and positioned herself between his legs. Gotti leaned forward enough to grab her waist and then pulled her down onto the couch next to him. He adjusted her body, lowering her on her back, and took both her thighs, moving his hands across her skin until they reached her waist again.

Najah just stared at him, not knowing what to expect. When he lowered his head between her legs and spread her thighs, she damn near lost it.

Just like that, his tongue was invading her center and digging in like he was on a mission. He kissed, sucked, and licked every inch while her eyes rolled back in her head and she bit her lip, trying to control the urge to scream out. Instead, she tried to push him away by placing her hands on his shoulders, but it was pointless. His large hands held her firmly in place, showing no mercy. When he eventually lifted his head and she felt like she had a moment of relief, his fingers entered her and he began to suck on her swollen clit.

Najah was done for. She gave up and turned her body over to him. Within minutes of giving him control, she felt a wave hit her and she released so hard that every muscle in her body ached from being so tight. Afterward, she lay there panting with her eyes closed, trying to get a grip. She was afraid to open them because she could feel Gotti staring at her.

When she eventually did, she was right, his eyes were on her and his expression was hard, making the situation more uncomfortable.

She yanked at the hem of the shirt she was wearing to cover herself and scooted back.

"You still wanna go home?" he asked as he stood and looked at her, still with no real readable expression.

"Is that why I'm here?"

He laughed arrogantly. "Nah, you're here because I wanted you near me. That shit right there was because a I needed to make a point."

"And what point is that?"

"Do you like how I make you feel?"

Najh looked at him like he was crazy. She was starting to question his sanity. He was all over the place with the way he was acting.

"Yeah, but what does that have to do with anything?" she said and rolled her eyes, annoyed that he was acting so unpredictable.

"It has to do with everything. Your little ass was in that damn club going hard for Joy about some bullshit that you weren't even involved in. That was your brother and Joy's shit, so how the fuck you gonna act when some female fronts you about me? When she gets in your damn face questioning you because she liked the way I used to make her feel. I'm not with all that hood shit, Najah."

She didn't know how to respond, so she didn't, but he did.

"That's exactly why I said you need to get your head right before I fuck with you. 'Cause once I give you all of me, everything changes, and I'm not fucking with you if you can't handle that."

"I can handle it," Najah said, looking him right in his eyes. She knew her temper and she knew from past experiences with Fezz that she was likely telling a lie, but she wanted Gotti, and wasn't about to let him walk away.

"I hope you mean that shit because I'm dead ass. I'm not fucking around with all that drama and nonsense. If you with me then you know you with me, and nobody should be able to make you question that."

Najah scooted to the edge of the sofa before she let her feet hit the floor and stood.

"Fine, but don't take that to mean that you can be doing shit behind my back just because you expect me not to question you. I'm not going to be anybody's fool." She sighed.

Gotti smiled and pulled her to him. He towered over her, which he loved. Gotti had always had a thing for short women.

"I'm not a cheater, ma. If I'm riding with you, I'm riding with you. Not saying I'm perfect, and I might fuck up from time to time, but if you're loyal to me then I got you. That's all you need to know."

Najah smiled as she looked up into his eyes. His words were sincere and she believed him, so for now, she was giving him a chance.

"Now, you still wanna leave?" Gotti asked with a smirk.

"And what if I do?"

He laughed. "Man, fuck that. We're about to go to bed. I'm tired as fuck, and I know your ass don't wanna go nowhere."

Gotti lifted Najah off the ground and she secured her legs around his waist. He held her in place with ease before kissing her neck and then her lips. He carried Najah to his room, where he placed her on this bed and then stepped out of his sweat pants.

"You still don't get this shit until I know you're ready, so keep your hands to yourself."

Gotti winked before he firmly grasped what was pressed against his thigh.

Najah rolled her eyes and crawled to the top of his bed. She pulled the covers back and then positioned her body underneath them.

After he was in bed next to her, he pulled her body against his chest and slid his hand between her thighs. Just like that, he was caressing her again, rubbing and stroking her insides, letting his fingers glide in and out of her. Najah closed her eyes and enjoyed his touch. After a few minutes, his motions slowed down and then stopped. Najah could feel his breathing slowing down, so she knew he had gone to sleep.

She rolled her eyes and tried to move his hand, but he held it in place. "Chill, man," he mumbled against her neck, so she let it go.

"This fool is about to go to sleep with his fingers in my shit," she whispered and sighed.

After a few minutes passed, Gotti spoke again. His voice vibrated against her back, startling her because she was almost asleep and assumed he was too.

"You said you riding with me, so this is my shit. I'll leave them bitches wherever the fuck I want, now take your ass to sleep."

She laughed and shook her head. What was she supposed to say to that?

\*\*\*\*\*

Logic watched Joy as she moved around his room gathering all of her things. She had stuff everywhere, which he was still getting used to, but he didn't mind. The tiny shorts she was wearing held his attention while he was supposed to be counting money. It was on the floor in front of him in neatly stacked piles.

"Why do you keep so much cash here?" Joy asked, standing in front of him with her hands on her hips.

His eyes moved up her legs right to her center before he bit his bottom lip.

"I just do. I get income from Intrigued, so that shit goes in the bank, but I can't really justify having this much cash. I put it in the bank in small amounts so that it doesn't draw too much attention."

Joy eyed the stacks of green fifties, hundreds, tens, ones and fives. She knew it was a lot. But she was curious about just how much, so that was her next question.

"How much is that?" Joy asked.

"Why, you gone hit me for it?" Logic asked with a grin.

A smirk formed as she stared down at him. "If I was going to steal from you I would have done that already. You gave me the code to your safe, remember?"

Logic chuckled. "Maybe I changed that shit already. I might not trust you."

"You trust me, or I wouldn't be here. So no, I'm not going to hit you for it. I have my own money. I don't need yours."

He smiled at how arrogantly she was speaking. "Chill, I know you do, but that little ass teacher's salary can't touch this."

"How much?"

"All together? Half a mil."

Joy's eyes bucked as she looked down to recheck the piles of cash. "Are you serious?"

"Yeah, why?"

"I don't know, that's a lot of money."

"It don't mean shit. It's just money. I mean, don't get me wrong, I like having it, but I don't get caught up in it. I wanna buy a house though." Logic watched Joy's face at the mention of buying a house. Technically, she was the inspiration behind it, so he was curious about how she would react.

He had been thinking about it for a minute, but things had been so crazy that there was never time to process it. Logic wasn't flashy; he liked nice things, but it didn't move him one way or another. The only reason he was considering the purchase of a house was because of Joy. He had paid her rent for the remainder of her lease since she spent most of her time at his place.

His apartment was small as hell, and he felt like Joy deserved more. She never complained. In fact, she seemed content with being at his place. But even if she was, he wanted her to have more than just his tiny ass apartment. The fact that she never complained made him want it for her even more.

"A house?"

He chuckled. "Yeah, why the fuck you say it like that?" Joy's tone was more questioning than confirming.

She grinned and shrugged. "I don't know. You just seem happy like you are. It doesn't really seem like your thing."

"There you go with that shit again. What's my thing, Joy?" He looked up at her and smiled.

"You know what I mean."

"Nah, I don't. Explain." He was only teasing; he knew what she meant.

"I mean you don't spend a lot of money, and you're just kind of you. You have nice things, your clothes are expensive, but not in an over the top kind of way, and I don't know..."

"You calling me cheap, Joy?" Logic stood and positioned his body in front of hers but didn't touch her.

She laughed. "No, not at all. You're just not all about material stuff. I like that."

"You like that, huh?"

This time his hands gripped her waist and he stepped to her.

"Yeah, I do. I like a lot of things about you."

"Care to elaborate?" A smile spread across his face.

"Nope," she teased.

"That's not working for me, though," he said as his hands began to explore her body.

"How about I show you?"

Joy grinned and slid her hand into Logic's boxers. Once she found what she was looking for, she backed him toward the bed until he lowered his body against it. With her kneeling in front of him, she took him into her mouth and began to caress his manhood with her lips and tongue.

"Oh shit, Joy," Logic moaned as his fingers tangled in her hair.

When he felt the head hit the back of her throat, he grabbed a fist full of her hair, trying to control what he was feeling. It was only the third time she had pleased him, but after the second, when he guided and instructed her on how to satisfy him, she had quickly become an expert. Joy still struggled with his size a little, but he damn sure wasn't going to complain.

Logic lifted his head just enough to see Joy's mouth moving up and down his length. That did something to him because his nut was surfing fast and strong. He pushed her away and covered his throbbing erection with his hand, releasing so strong that it took him a minute before he could even move. He lay there with his hand covering his manhood, eyes closed, slowly recovering.

When his eyes eventually opened, Joy was watching him with a grin, which made him laugh.

"You think that shit is cute huh?" he asked, lifting his head just a little before letting it hit the bed again.

Joy smiled and left the room. She returned shortly after with a warm washcloth that she used to clean him up with. Once she was done, she tossed it on the dresser and then straddled his lap.

"How was that?" she questioned.

"Do you really have to ask?"

She shrugged and then leaned down to kiss him. After tugging slightly on his lips, she grinned. "Yeah."

Logic laughed. "You keep that shit up and not only will I buy you a house, but anything else you want too." He lifted his head to kiss her again.

"You don't have to buy me things because of that. I just want you to be happy." Joy bit her bottom lip and stared at him.

"I know that, and I am. I'm buying us a house because we can't have a family in this little ass shit." Logic winked at Joy and grinned.

"Family? Who says I want a family?"

"I did." His hand moved under her shirt and rested on her stomach. "You're having my baby, Joy. We already discussed that shit."

"Not we, you." Joy pointed to Logic and she laughed.

"Your memory is a little cloudy, but it doesn't matter. My baby will be in here soon." His hand moved across her stomach as he smiled thinking about it.

Joy shoved his hand away and lifted her body from his. "Jury's still out on that one." She lifted the pile of clothes that she had collected from around his room and dumped them in the hamper.

"Yeah, aight. We'll see about that," Logic said as he sat up to finish counting his money.

Joy's just shook her head and smiled. She knew he was serious, even if she wasn't. For now, she wasn't in any hurry to have a baby. Things were good with them and she liked it that way.

## -9-

Rah drove through the streets of Atlanta in the Range that Marilyn had allowed him to use, feeling at ease. He had been out of jail for a week and should have been gone, but Marilyn had him living like a king, and he wasn't quite ready to let go of that just yet. She had him up in an expensive ass suite downtown, access to an unlimited supply of cash, and driving around in a brand new Range. Why the hell should he be in a hurry to let that go?

She was working on his case and had made all types of promises to get it thrown out. No one knew where he was, and at this point, he was just chilling. Aside from the fact that Marilyn was acting like she owned him, shit was lovely. He didn't mind breaking her off because Marilyn knew how to please him, but he was tired of her already. Too much of anything could be a bad thing, and right now he needed a break from her, so he was heading across town to go check out a shorty he met a few days ago.

He thought about bringing her to his suite, but he knew that Marilyn had the potential to just pop up, and that was a problem he didn't need. He wasn't about to fuck up his free ride over a random female, especially one he had no plans to see again, so he was making the drive to see her instead.

When Rah pulled up at the location the shorty had given him, he looked around, feeling like he knew where he was. Like he had been there before, but he shook it off, parked and got out. He made sure to take his pistol with him, not trusting anyone, and he didn't really know this chick.

After he rang the bell, he leaned against the house and waited. A few minutes later, the door opened and she stood there grinning, barely dressed in a tank top and pair of spandex shorts. Her breasts were spilling out the top of her tank top because it was about two sizes too small, and she wasn't wearing a bra.

Rah's tongue glided across his bottom lip before he smiled. "Can I come in, or are we just gonna stand here staring at each other?" he asked, noticing the lustful look in her eyes.

She grinned but didn't say anything, just stepped back so that he could enter, which he did.

"You live alone?" he asked, looking around. The house was a bit much for one person. It was nicely decorated and well kept.

"Yeah, why?"

"Come on, baby, you know why. I don't have time for your man to be popping up on us while I got your legs in the air," Rah said.

He was there for one reason, and she knew that. If she didn't then he wanted it to be clear. This was strictly a fuck and go type situation. He didn't need, nor did he have time for anything else.

"We're safe. I don't have a man, unless you want to change that," she offered with a seductive smile.

Rah chuckled. "We'll see about that." He already knew the answer, but right now his goal was to fuck her senseless, and letting her know that was his only intention would make it difficult to do.

"What you got to sip on?" Rah asked, grabbing her slim waist and pulling her body to his. His hands moved down her butt and grabbed it firmly before he kissed her neck."

"I have a bottle of Hennessy," she offered.

"Aight, let's get that popping then, so I can get this popping." He moved his hand between her thighs.

She let out a soft moan from the way he touched her and then stepped back to lead the way to her bedroom. She stopped in the kitchen to grab the Hennessy and two glasses.

After she had downed one glass to Rah's two, he wasted no time undressing her. His hand moved quickly, exposing her body while he kissed and sucked her neck. She groped his sweatpants, massaging his erection that was already at its full potential while she enjoyed the feel of his hands on her body.

Rah reached in his pocket before stepping out of his shoes. He retrieved one of the condoms he had brought with him before she pushed his sweatpants and boxers down his body. Once she caught sight of what he was working with she got a little nervous, which showed on her face.

"You're good, ma, I'll be gentle," he said with a grin as he ripped open the condom and removed it from the wrapper.

She watched, still a little nervous. Once he had it in place, he reached for her waist and walked her backward to her bed.

"Get on your knees," he said as his hand moved around her neck and then down her breasts.

Once again, she hesitated, and Rah sighed before he explained, "I can enter you much better that way. You already looking like you're about to run."

She did as instructed and got on all fours. Rah was behind her and wasted no time entering her. Because of his size and the fact that she tensed up, he was struggling, so he rubbed her clit and kissed her back, trying to get her to ease up a little.

"Baby, you have to relax or I can't give you what you want," he said with irritation. He was ready to fuck, and she was playing around.

"I'm trying, but damn baby, you're making it hard."

"I got you, just relax."

Again, he pushed forward, and this time he made it halfway. He pulled out again and then rammed into her, losing patience, forcing her body to move forward and she yelled out a little from the impact.

"Wait, please wait. I just need a minute."

"Nah, just let me handle it. Once I get going, you'll be good." Rah grabbed her around the waist and held her tight while he moved slowly in and out of her body.

She relaxed a little and he could tell that she was beginning to enjoy herself, so he closed his eyes and went to work. He planned to get a quick nut and then get the hell out of there.

"So, when can I see you again?"

Rah looked back over his shoulder as he stepped into his Nikes. He was sitting on the foot of her bed while she lay across it behind him, still naked. Her curves stood out because she was on her side with her head propped up in her hand while her elbow held her up.

He just smiled, but didn't answer.

"I know you hear me," she said with a little aggression before sitting up.

Rah stood and turned to face her with his arms folded across his chest.

"I hear you, but let's just call this what it is. A good fuck. I know you're not expecting more than that."

Her face turned hard and she got angry.

"Nigga, I'm not a hoe. I don't just sleep with random people for the hell of it. You're here because you acted like you were looking to chill."

Rah laughed. "How the fuck did I act like I wanted more than what you just gave me? I met you at a damn restaurant. Told you that you look like you taste sweet, and you gave me your number. I didn't say shit about trying to kick it. That's your fault if you thought that because I damn sure didn't tell you that in any kind of way. You knew the deal because when I got here today, your ass was half dressed, licking your damn lips and then opened your legs without so much as a conversation. This was a quick nut, sweetheart. You knew that shit the second you opened your front door."

She jumped up and rushed him, but he grabbed her wrist and shoved her back toward the bed, causing her to land on her back.

"Yo, don't be stupid," Rah growled through gritted teeth.

"Fuck you. I swear, I'll fuck you up."

She jumped up again, but he grabbed her by the neck and squeezed until her eyes began to roll back in her head. She clawed at his hands, trying to free herself, on the verge of passing out. Not wanting a body on his hands, he quickly got it together and let her go. She fell to the floor, gasping for air as tears left her eyes.

"You're crazy," she whispered, unable to fully speak because of what he had done.

Rah smiled. "Yeah, I am, so if I were you, I would forget all 'bout this. You never know just how crazy I am, and I don't think you want to find out." He reached in his pocket and pulled out a fold of cash that Marilyn had blessed him with. He removed two hundreds and tossed them on the floor.

"Take care, ma." He winked at her before he left her room.

Once he was out the front door, he noticed something that quickly made him remember why the neighborhood that he was in felt familiar. Joy pulled out of a driveway across the street; it was Karma's house. He had been there with Joy once, years ago. He quickly made his way to Marilyn's Range so that he could follow her. *Could shit get any better?* he thought as he rubbed his chin and pulled away from the curb.

*****

"I just left. I'm going to grab us something to eat and then I'll be home."

Joy smiled as she mentioned the word *home*. Even after all the time that she and Logic had been together, it still felt weird to Joy that Logic was home to her. Weird but right. It was comfortable, but still odd at times. She was so caught up in her conversation that she didn't realize Rah was following her. She wouldn't have anyway, because she didn't pay attention to things like that.

"Good, hurry up. I miss you, damn. You just left me hanging. I woke up and you were gone."

Joy grinned, thinking about the fact that she'd chosen not to wake Logic from his nap. Over the last week, he had been working so hard, in late and up early. She heard conversations that he had with Gotti about how business was picking up, so the two of them were on the block literally all day and night. Most of the information she had about what was going on with Logic in the streets, she found out from Najah. Logic didn't really discuss that part of his life with her, but she didn't care. Joy knew where he was, and as long as he came home to her every night, then it didn't matter to her one way or the other.

"You were tired and you knew I had plans with Karma, so there was no point in waking you."

He laughed. "Yeah, aight, you just didn't want me to be up in your shit before you left, that's all. You ain't slick, but I got you when you get here."

Now Joy laughed. "It didn't have anything to do with that, I just knew you were tired." Joy partially lied.

Logic had been on a mission lately. He couldn't keep his hands off her, which she knew was about him trying to get her pregnant. The two of them had searched and saved several houses that they wanted to look at, but because Logic had been so busy lately, they hadn't gotten a chance to go see any of them. But he made it clear that he wanted a baby to go along with the house that he was buying.

Joy pulled into the parking lot of her favorite soul food place and parked, with Rah right behind her. She shut off her car and reached for her purse, still having no clue that he had been following her.

"Just hurry up. I'm hungry, and I damn sure ain't talking about that food you're about to order." Logic's confession made Joy blush as she unlocked her door to get out, but the second she did, she instantly regretted it.

"Hey, baby. Damn, I missed you." Rah's voice made the hair on her neck stand up.

"Who the fuck is that?" Logic yelled so loud through the phone that Joy knew for sure Rah heard it.

The grin on his face as he peered down at her and snatched her phone from her hands was confirmation. With his pistol pointed at Joy, Rah shook his head to tell her no when he realized that she was about to try to take it back.

"You know who the fuck this is, and I'm hanging up now. Joy and I have some catching up to do." Rah ended the call and tossed her phone into the car before he grabbed Joy's arm.

"Let's go," he said with a smirk.

"I'm not going with you. You must be crazy." Joy snatched away but was unsuccessful in freeing herself from his grasp.

"Look, I don't have time for this shit. I love you, Joy, but don't think I won't shoot your ass. Now stop fucking around and let's go."

Joy noticed the deranged look in Rah's eyes and then the gun he had pressed against her side, and decided it wasn't worth fighting him over. He was so unpredictable that she didn't know what he was capable of. At that point, all Joy could think about was staying alive, and she knew that Logic was likely going crazy. If she went with Rah, there was a possibility that she could talk him down and get away from him, but dying wasn't an option, so she gave in.

He held her tight until they reached a black Range Rover that looked familiar to Joy. She was praying that it didn't belong to who she thought. Rah pointed to the driver's side and she pulled the door and got in. Once she got in, she realized from the monogrammed seats that it was her mother's truck, which infuriated her. She just didn't understand her mother.

"Why are you driving my mother's truck?" Joy snapped.

"That's none of your damn business, just drive." He pointed to the steering wheel.

"And just where do you think we're going?"

Joy watched him and knew that he was thinking, which meant that he hadn't thought things through. That made her even more nervous because Rah was acting off emotion and that was dangerous.

"Go to your place."

"Logic's there," Joy lied.

Rah laughed. "I know you, Joy. It's been awhile, but I still know you. Go to your damn apartment. That nigga ain't there, I can see it in your eyes. And if he is, I'll just shoot him too." Rah grinned, which pissed Joy off.

She didn't know what was about to happen, but she had a feeling it wasn't going to be good.

# -10-

Logic was out the door before he could even think straight about his plan. As soon as he backed out of the parking space and ripped into the street, his phone was to his ear and dialing Joy again. With every ring, his heart pounded harder in his chest. When her voice picked up, telling him to leave a message, he felt like his heart stopped completely, each and every time he dialed and heard it.

"Fuck, fuck, fuck." He yelled after tossing his phone into the passenger seat. He had no idea what his first move should be, but he knew exactly where he was going.

The entire thirty-minute drive to Joy's parents' house was torture. Every second of knowing that Rah had Joy made his pulse race because all he could think about was what he was doing to her. The worst thoughts filled his head and it infuriated him.

When Logic arrived at Joy's parents' house, he jumped out the car moving straight to the door with murder on his mind. His hand met the expensive wood with so much force that pain shot through it and he continued beating on the door until her father appeared, wearing a scowl that matched Logic's frustration.

"Where the fuck is she?" Within seconds, Logic had his gun pressed against Lionel's forehead, backing him into his home.

Logic kicked the door shut from behind, but kept his eyes on Joy's father.

"She should be with you. You know she's not here and that's because of you. What did you do to my daughter? Did you finally show her who you really are?"

"Man, shut the fuck up with all that. Your daughter? That's a got damn joke, you don't own the right to call her that. I'm looking for your trifling ass wife, so you find her or I shoot you and find her my damn self."

"What is going on?" Marilyn's voice flowed from the top of the stairs as she moved down them like she owned the world.

The second she hit the last step, Logic rocked the shit out of Joys father and rushed Marilyn. His hand moved to her neck, shoving his gun in her mouth and her eyes bucked to the point where they should have popped out of her head.

Logic could hear Joy's father moving behind him, so he tightened his hold around Marilyn's neck to keep her contained, and pointed his gun at Lionel. "Get your ass over here before you do something that will cost you your life and this bitch hers. At this point, I don't really give a fuck."

"You know you're going to jail, right?" Lionel wore a smirk as he held the eye that was quickly swelling due to the impact that Logic's fist had made with it.

Logic chuckled as Lionel stood there peering at him. "Not if I kill your bitch ass first. Now get the fuck over here. I don't have time to play with your insignificant ass. Your daughter's safety might not mean shit to you, but it means everything to me, and you're wasting my got damn time."

For the first time, Lionel realized the wild look in Logic's eyes and moved toward him. Logic nodded toward the stairs in front of him. Lionel moved up two and positioned himself behind Marilyn.

"Now, where the fuck is he?"

"I don't know what you're talking about." Marilyn lied.

She knew that Logic was talking about Rah, but she wasn't about to let that be known. Not while her husband was standing there. Lionel still had no clue that she had bailed him out of jail and that she was hiding him away in return for sex.

Logic let out an evil laugh as he began to squeeze harder, causing Marilyn to gasp for air.

"Bitch, I will snap your neck. Now keep fucking playing.

"Who are you looking for and why do you think my wife knows where they are?" Logic looked up at Lionel with a scowl. He had yet to defend his wife, but he felt the need to question Logic.

"Because this crazy bitch is fucking him. I guess you're too busy running after your new bitch and her son to take care of home or worry about the fact that your wife put someone on the streets that wants to hurt Joy."

Logic watched Lionel's face transition from confusion to anger before he focused on his wife, who was still struggling to breathe.

"What did you do?" he asked.

Marilyn looked at her husband with disgust before she focused on Logic, choosing to ignore her husband. She hadn't missed the fact that Logic mentioned him having a new woman and son. Marilyn had always suspected, but now it was confirmed.

"I don't know where he is."

Again, Logic let out an impatient laugh, in an effort to keep calm. As much as he wanted to kill both of them, he needed Marilyn's help to locate Joy first. She was all he had at this point, but he damn sure wasn't about to let her know that.

"Okay then." He cocked the hammer of his gun and was in the process of shoving it back into her mouth before she stopped him.

"Wait, please wait. I can track the truck that he's in," she released, barely audible because of the hold that Logic had on her.

He yanked her up by her neck and then looked her dead in the eyes. "Talk, and talk fast because whatever he does to her, I do to you, and it will be ten times worse."

"I can track it. I had something installed to track it." She glanced at her husband whose eyes darted back and forth between her and Logic.

"What the fuck is he talking about, Marilyn? What truck and who is he looking for?"

Logic didn't have time for them to be figure out which one was more fucked up, all he needed was a way to find Joy.

"Your dumb ass wife here got her little boyfriend out of jail and he just took your daughter. I don't know how the fuck Joy was raised by the two of you and managed to end up normal, but I know it didn't have shit to do with either one of you sick bastards."

He looked at Marilyn again. "Find him now."

"I have to get my phone. It's upstairs," she said.

"Are you still fucking him? You're a stupid bitch. Sleeping with him is bad enough, but you got him out of jail? What is wrong with you? Are you trying to ruin your career?" Lionel peered at his wife in disbelief.

"Nigga please, this bitch is fucking your daughter's ex-boyfriend and you're fucking some twenty-two-year-old that you have a son with, and all you can think about is her got damn career? Both y'all asses are crazy. Upstairs, let's go."

Logic kept his hold on Marilyn while he damn near dragged her up the stairs with his gun pointed at Lionel. When they reached their bedroom, he allowed Marilyn to get her phone and she pulled up the app that she had installed to track the truck that she had given to Rah. She didn't trust him, so she had a tracking system installed to make sure he was playing by her rules.

"Here." She held it up and Logic quickly realized the location. That was all he needed, so he released his hold on Marilyn and snatched her phone from her hand, but her dumb ass couldn't leave well enough alone.

"You better not kill him," she yelled, taking a step toward Logic, who at this point had had enough.

He turned and swung on her with so much force that her body spun just a little before she hit the bed and then the floor. He had never once hit a female in his life, but with Marilyn, he had no regrets.

She stumbled to her feet and looked at Lionel. "Are you going to just stand there?" she yelled.

Her question was apparently humorous to him because he laughed and pointed at his wife.

"You better hope he kills that nigga because if he doesn't I will, you stupid whore. I should have left your ass years ago. You are such an embarrassment."

"I'm an embarrassment, but you have a child with a twenty-two-year-old?" Marilyn laughed sarcastically while holding her face.

Logic couldn't believe those two. He didn't have time to deal with either one, so he left with them yelling at each other behind him, but just before he hit the door he stopped.

"Fuck with me if you want to and watch what happens. Jail don't mean shit to me if it means keeping Joy away from both you sick muthafuckers."

That got their attention and they both turned to him with a type of fear and understanding that let him know that he didn't have to worry about either of them. They were too wrapped up in their own insanity to worry about him or their daughter. Not once had either of them shown any concern for the fact that Rah had Joy, so Logic didn't really give a damn about killing them if they decided that they wanted to give him any problems.

*****

Rah's eyes roamed Joy's body as his tongue glided across his bottom lip. They were in her bedroom with him standing over the bed while she sat on the edge peering at him.

"Why the fuck you keep looking at that door? That nigga ain't coming. Can't nobody save you but me, Joy. I'm all you have, just like it's supposed to be. In the end, it all comes back to you and me, so quit fucking stalling and come up out that shit." Rah smirked as he looked down at Joy.

"You wanna shoot me, Rah? Then do it. I don't care anymore." Joy was afraid, but not enough to give in and have sex with him. He would have to shoot her first.

"That nigga got your head that damn gone that you'd rather die than give me what's mine? You're mine, Joy, always have been. He's temporary, and as much as I hate that you gave him what belongs to me, I can get over it. The second I slide up in you again, you'll remember who it belongs to, who you belong to."

Rah reached for Joy and grabbed her arm. She tried to snatch away, but he pulled her into his chest and covered her mouth with his. When she attempted to turn away, he tossed his gun onto the bed, knowing that he could overpower her with his strength and size. He grabbed her chin and forced another kiss on her.

"You can fight it all you want, shorty. I'm taking what's mine, with or without your permission. I'm gonna make you remember who you belong to and then kill that nigga you call yourself in love with."

Joy's eyes were filled with so much hate as they met his, but that only made him more driven. His eyes were dark and cold, and she didn't even recognize the person he had become. It was hard for her to believe that at some point she had actually loved him, because right now, witnessing the psychotic break that he was having, she had no idea who he was, and it had her at a loss.

When Rah's hand made it to her jeans and began to unfasten them, Joy fought hard against the hold he had on her. She tried to free herself, but it was pointless. Rah had one of her arms securely against his chest to hold her in place while her other grasped at his, trying to stop him from unbuckling her pants. When he had enough of Joy fighting against him, he grabbed her around the neck and shoved her into the wall.

"I don't want to hurt you, Joy, but I will. You need to stop fighting me and make this easy on yourself. You know you want it, so stop fighting me, Joy."

"If you really believe that, then you're just as crazy as you look," Joy yelled with her eyes on his.

He wasn't fazed in the least. In fact, it turned him on. He brought his lips to hers and tried to kiss her again while forcing his hand into her jeans. His fingers worked their way inside her and Joy's body tensed.

"See you like that shit, don't you, Joy?"

"I hate you. I fucking hate you." Joy continued to fight with his hand, but he shoved his fingers deeper inside her.

Joy closed her eyes to hold back the tears that were fighting their way to the surface. She wasn't going to cry. She refused to let him see her cry, and she refused to give in. Rah would have to fight her for anything he thought that he was about to get from her. Joy's eyes popped open when she felt her body jerk forward and Rah being snatched away from hers. She caught Logic's eyes as he threw Rah to the floor and started beating him so severely that she froze.

The wild look in Logic's eyes and the way he connected with Rah's body scared her just a little because he was beating him so severely that Rah didn't even have a chance to fight back. Joy watched as Logic took Rah's life, blow by blow, literally killing him with his bare hands. He delivered one hit after another, not stopping even after Rah took his last breath and lay lifeless on Joy's bedroom floor. In fact, Logic didn't snap out of it until he felt her hand on his shoulder.

With eyes full of rage, he looked up at her and they softened just a little before he stood and pulled her into his chest.

"I'm fine," Joy whispered into his body as he held her so tight that she couldn't move.

"This shit is on me, Joy, I keep fucking up with you."

"No, you don't. Don't do that, I'm fine. Let's just go."

She didn't want him for one minute to think that she was disappointed or felt like he wasn't keeping her safe. As much as he tried, there was no way to prevent everything, and she understood that.

"We can't do that yet. I need to make some calls." Logic kissed Joy's forehead and then held onto her for a few minutes more before he loosened his hold on her, just enough to see her face.

With a few kisses on her face and lips, he let her go and pulled his phone out of his pocket. This wasn't like any other body. It was Joy's ex-boyfriend dead in her apartment. That was going to cause a lot of questions that led right back to both of them, so they couldn't just walk away.

"How did you know where I was?" Things had calmed down enough for Joy to think, and her first thought was the fact that Logic was there.

His eyes turned dark again as they looked at Joy's because murderous thoughts about Marilyn had returned.

"Your mother," was all he said before he turned his back and focused on his call. "I need your help."

Joy waited while he spoke and she listened, trying to figure out who he was talking to and why. After a few minutes, Logic rattled off her address before he ended the call and pulled her to the living room. She looked around and noticed the door wide open with Logic's keys still in the lock. Her mind was spinning, and she felt like she was in a daze, but the second she felt his arms around her again, everything calmed.

*****

Logic looked around Joy's bedroom while Luther explained what happened to the detective he had called in favor to. How Rah grabbed Joy, brought her to her apartment, and was on the verge of assaulting her before Logic showed up. The men fought and Rah ended up dead.

"Self-defense, huh?" Downs asked again as he turned his attention from Luther to Logic.

He scanned Logic's body in search of at least one sign that the men had an altercation. Rah was barely recognizable, and aside from light bruising and blood on Logic's clothes and hands, there wasn't a mark on him that indicated that he been attacked. The altercation appeared to be extremely one sided.

"Self-defense, Downs," Luther said firmly, knowing exactly what Downs had to be thinking. "I need you to make this go away. You know I don't pull rank or make demands, that's not who I am, but this is important. You owe me, and I need you to make this go away, so self-defense."

Luther glanced at Logic before he laid eyes on Downs again. Downs looked at Luther first, then Logic, before he scanned the room. He walked over to the bed and lifted the gun that belonged to Rah by the barrel and handed it to Logic.

"I assume you can make this disappear?"

Logic nodded, took the gun and slid it under his shirt and into the waist band of his jeans.

"I need to get a statement. After that, you're free to go. I can call in a few favors to get the body processed without any one asking questions, so we should be in the clear. I'll make it go away. After this, we're even." He was now looking at Luther.

Downs had been Luther's partner for a few years before Luther retired. He owed Luther for covering up a body for him after things got out of control one night at a bar. Downs had too much to drink and beat a guy to death who claimed to be sleeping with his wife. Turns out it was true, but Luther helped Downs get rid of the body, so no one ever found out. Making this situation go a way for Logic was repayment for that, and Downs was glad to return the favor. He respected Luther and appreciated what he had done for him.

Luther extended a hand to Downs and the two men shook on it. Logic did the same and then left. Luther and Downs got to work on the details while he went back to living room where Joy was. The second he hit the corner, her eyes were on him and she tried to smile, but he could see the stress on her face.

Logic sat down next to Joy on the sofa and lowered his arm around her shoulders, forcing her into his side.

"Why are they here?" She asked, confused about why Logic had called Luther who showed up with someone who she knew was a cop.

"This is your apartment, Joy, and that's your ex-boyfriend. All this shit is in your name. We couldn't leave a body here without there being a million questions why. They're taking care of that so that it doesn't come back on you."

"Me, what about you? They'll know I didn't do that so they'll assume it was you."

Logic smiled at the fact that she was more worried about him than she was about herself. "I'm good. They have it under control."

"But that's a cop, don't they have to—"

"No, they don't have to do anything that will come back to either one of us. It's handled. I'm not going anywhere and neither are you. When we walk out of here, this shit is over. Get whatever you need before you leave because you're never coming back."

She looked at Logic, wanting to question him more, but decided against it. Rah was gone, and Logic had assured her that she didn't have to worry about the fact that he took Rah's life. The details weren't important. As long as they could move on, she had no problem letting it go.

# -11-

"Yo, you good?" Gotti asked as he eyed Logic.

Logic and Gotti were sitting in his car behind an abandoned warehouse, which was one of the locations they used to do handoffs. Logic made a point of always switching things up because he didn't have a lot of trust in people, especially Solomon, who they were currently waiting for to get their product.

"Yeah, why, what's up?" Logic slid his phone back into his pocket and looked up at Gotti.

"You keep checking your phone and shit, like you waiting on something. I got this if you need to jet."

Logic laughed when me realized Gotti was right. Ever since the situation had gone down with Rah, he had Joy checking in with him damn near all day. It was almost three o'clock, which meant that school would be letting out and he should be receiving a text from her at any minute to let him know that she was good and on her way to Mini's house. She was supposed to head there straight there from her school at Mini's request to help her cook for the family dinner. Logic was happy about Joy and his mother's relationship. The two talked all the time, and Joy even went there to spend time with Mini without him.

"Nah, I'm good, and there goes Solomon anyway." Logic looked up at the three Black SUVs that pulled into the parking lot where they were waiting. He and Gotti both got out, leaned against his car, and waited for Solomon to approach. Logic's mind was on the fact that he was about to piss Solomon off, so a cocky grin was plastered on his face as they watched the vehicles that had just arrived.

A few minutes later, Solomon approached and the men shook hands just before Solomon began to speak.

"This is a large order. I take it this has something to do with the area you took over from Rah and his brother. It's a shame they just disappeared like that. First Donte and Fezz, and now Rah and Moses."

Solomon wore a smirk as he glanced at Logic after hinting around to Logic's involvement in the four men's disappearance. Gotti picked up on it and moved his hand under his shirt. Logic already wasn't feeling Solomon, and trying to send verbal shots at him was definitely not the move, or helping the situation. In fact, the only reason Logic had tolerated Solomon all this time was because they got quality product for a decent price, but that was about to change. With the increase in what they were ordering, Levi, who was Solomon's boss, had reached out to Logic and offered him a better deal.

Logic cut his eyes at Solomon before holding his hand up to stop him from talking. Logic's gesture was purposely disrespectful, handling Solomon like a child who was speaking out of turn, which made Gotti chuckle. Logic pulled his phone out of his pocket, read a message from Joy, responded, and then slid it back into his pocket before he looked up to focus on Solomon again.

"Yeah, seems like people just be disappearing and shit. The funny thing is, it's always somebody who tried some disrespectful shit with me. That's just crazy as fuck. What do you think, Solomon?" Logic wore a cocky grin after his low key threat.

He could see the tension lines forming on Solomon's face because he knew that Logic was sending him a message. Solomon wasn't really a threat; he was just a man who had lucked up on an opportunity. After speaking to Levi, Logic was informed that Solomon was fucking up and wouldn't be around much longer.

"Coincidence, I guess." Solomon glanced across his shoulder where his men were standing before addressing Logic again. "So, I was thinking that with this new territory you have, it might be a good idea to renegotiate. I feel like we could come to some better terms and help you make a lot more money. With a little more commitment on your end, we could probably get you a much better deal than you have now."

Logic looked at him with no expression. "Oh yeah? More commitment on my end, huh?"

"Absolutely. You're a loyal customer, so it's only right."

A cocky grin formed on Logic's face as he peered at Solomon. "Only right, huh? See, the problem I have with that is that you already promised me that I was getting the best deal possible, and now here you are, telling me that I'm not. How the fuck should I feel about that, since I'm such a loyal customer? What I think is that you did some math and are now trying to cash in on my expansion. I'm a lot of things, but stupid is not one of them. I don't know, seems to me like I might need to start shopping around my damn self. Maybe I'll just reach out to Levi. That's your boss, right? What you think about that, Gotti?" Logic looked at his partner.

"Aye, sounds like a good idea to me. I mean, if this nigga can't respect you enough to give you the best value for your money, then find someone who will." Gotti looked at Solomon and grinned.

Solomon looked at Logic and then got pissed, but he knew he couldn't really say shit. He had made a lot of money off them and didn't want to lose their business. Also, the fact that Logic had mentioned Levi made him nervous, and since they were now buying triple the product, he backed down. A buy like theirs should have gone through Levi anyway, and he knew it.

"I see. I guess we're good like we are?" He glanced over his shoulder before waving his hand in the air.

Two men stepped out of one of the SUVs carrying two oversized duffle bags and headed their way. Logic opened his trunk and retrieved a backpack full of money. They did their exchange and Gotti loaded the product in the trunk.

"So, I guess I'll hear from you soon. You guys are moving through product faster than I really expected," Solomon said, trying to gauge Logic's mood. He knew he had fucked up and was trying to regain a little.

Logic glanced at him and made his way to the driver's side of his car. He pulled the door and got in without responding.

To further make it clear that he had no respect for Solomon, he smiled and casually tossed out, "Maybe, I'll have to think about that."

"Yo, you just pissed him the fuck off," Gotti said and laughed. "Got that nigga sweating and shit, thinking we're 'bout to bail on his ass."

Logic looked at Gotti as he pulled off. He hadn't discussed with him the conversation he had with Levi yet. "We are."

"Word, what's fucking up with that?" Gotti rubbed his hands together before he looked Logic's way.

"The only reason I fucked with Solomon in the first place was because I couldn't get to his plug. Fuck him. We're going straight to the source now. Levi wouldn't fuck with people unless you were dealing in big numbers. With Rah's territory, we got that shit easy."

"Yo, I told your ass, this right here is where you need to be." Gotti leaned back and laughed.

Not long after, the two were back at their spot in the basement watching over a few of their guys as they got the product they had just picked up ready to hit the street.

"You now my moms is about to be all in your shit about my sister, right?" Logic said after reading a text from Joy, telling him that they were done cooking.

"For what?"

"Cause, bruh, you're kicking it with her baby girl. She don't take that shit too light."

Gotti laughed as he lifted the blunt he was holding and lit it. "I ain't worried about that. Moms love me," Gotti insisted, which made Logic laugh.

"Shit, that just because you never had to deal with Mini. She goes hard, yo. Especially when it comes to Najah. That's her baby girl, and after Fezz, she be looking at everybody with a side eye."

Gotti smirked. "Man, I got this. Your mom was cool as hell the first time I met her. She was going in on your ass, but she was cool with me."

Gotti thought about how Mini was pissed at Logic for taking over her house and forcing everyone to stay there the night he couldn't get his hands on Rah. Mini had been nice to him, offering him food and making sure he had what he needed to be comfortable for the night.

"Don't let that shit fool you. That was before she knew you were fucking with her daughter. You and Nah Nah are on some couple type shit now, and that's a game changer, bruh. Just wait."

"Man, Najah is grown," Gotti said before he released a cloud of smoke.

"Walk your ass in there telling Mini that shit, and you better fucking run. And I suggest you don't show up smelling like that shit or she's really going in on your ass."

Gotti held his blunt out and looked at it. "I feel you. I'll be straight, but your ass better have my damn back."

"Hell fucking no. That's your shit, bruh. I ain't fucking with Mini like that so she can go in on me." Logic shook his head and laughed.

"Yo, that's fucked up, man."

"You my people and everything, but when it comes to Mini, it's every man for himself."

Now Gotti was shaking his head. He hoped things went smoothly because he was feeling Najah. Since Moses and Rah were handled and business was picking up, it was time to get his personal life in order, which meant locking shit down with Najah. He didn't think that meant getting past her mother, but if that was what needed to be done, then fuck it. Let the games begin.

*****

Nova looked up at Nathan as she stepped out the shower, lifted her towel off the rack, and wrapped it around her body. He was standing in the doorway watching her with his arms folded across his chest.

"You're really making this no sex thing hard, especially when you're looking like that."

She eyed his handsome face and grinned. "That's your fault. I didn't ask you to come in here, did I?"

Nate stepped into the bathroom and wrapped his arms around Nova before kissing her neck.

"I couldn't help it. How do you expect me to know that you're in here naked and not take a peek?"

"Then that's on you," Nova said and moved past him to leave the bathroom.

She and Nate had been kicking it for a few weeks, but unlike her other relationships, she decided to slow things down a little. After dealing with Rah, she learned that people aren't always what they seem, and she wasn't interested in finding that out the hard way again.

The night after she met Nate at the club, he had called her. They talked for hours and she had an instant attraction. He was taking some getting used to because he was not like the guys that she usually dated, but she was committed to really giving him a chance. Nate was a legit businessman. He was a lawyer and not from the streets, which was a one eighty from the men she usually dated.

At twenty-eight years old, he owned his own home, didn't rely on anyone but himself, and didn't have any kids or crazy exes. She couldn't really understand why he was hanging in there with her because she was a typical single mom struggling to figure out life, but none of that seemed to matter with him. Every time she questioned him about it, he just said that he saw something in her.

"So, why are you so secretive about this family dinner? You hiding me or something? Am I not good enough to meet your family?"

Nova slipped into her panties before turning her back to him and putting on her bra. After she was done, she tossed her towel on the bed and pulled her closet door open to find something to wear.

"I'm not secretive about it. If I was, you wouldn't even know about it. It's not about hiding you, things are just complicated with my family," Nova admitted before selecting a pair of jeans and then stepping into them.

Nate looked at her with concern. "Complicated how? All families are complicated, mine included."

He sat on her bed facing her as she pulled her shirt over her head. Once she adjusted it around her body, she stood in front of him, trying to decide how to explain that her cousin was a drug dealer, one of the biggest in their area, and him being a lawyer didn't have her feeling all warm and fuzzy inside about the two crossing paths. Lawyers weren't cops, but they worked hand and hand.

"The last time I brought a guy to meet my family, he and my cousin ended up almost shooting each other, so maybe it's not such a good idea for you to meet them," she teased, trying to bring humor into the situation.

The look on Nate's face let her know that he wasn't really sure how to respond, so she stood there waiting until he eventually did.

"Look, I don't know what that's about, but I would assume it had something to do with you choosing the wrong guy. I like you. I like your kids. I want more of you, and that means more of who you are. I don't care who your family is or what they do. I'm a corporate lawyer, not a criminal one, and even if I was, my business is my business and yours is yours. If I meet your family then it's Nate, the man who is under Nova's spell, not Nate, the corporate lawyer. Don't hide from me because you think I might complicate things or judge. I just want more of you, that's it."

Nova stood there processing his words, not really knowing where to go from there. One thing was for sure, she was definitely feeling Nate, and she hoped that things would continue to grow. Maybe it wouldn't be so bad to bring him into their circle. If nothing else, she knew that they would let her know their thoughts on him. Nova still didn't one hundred percent trust her judgment, so having Nate around her family, might actually work out to be a good thing.

"Fine, but don't say I didn't warn you."

A grin spread across her face as she stepped between his legs. His hands held the back of her thighs and she leaned down to connect her lips with his. He returned the favor and Nova said a silent prayer that they could make it through dinner without any guns involved.

# -12-

Joy sat in Logic's lap with her arms around his neck, while his rested on her body. One on her thigh, the other under her shirt on her stomach. She was all smiles as she watched Najah squirm while Mini and Luther played twenty questions with Gotti, who wore a soft smile, not really moved by the interrogation that they were putting him through.

"She's more stressed than he is," Joy whispered against Logic's ear before she kissed the side of his face.

"I know, which means that she really likes his ass. Otherwise, she wouldn't give a fuck." Logic kissed Joy's neck and then moved one of his fingers into the waist band of her jeans, but he stopped there since he and Joy weren't alone in the kitchen.

"And you're how old?" Mini asked for the third time like she was expecting Gotti to change his answer.

He chuckled before winking at Najah, who was across the room from where he was standing. "Twenty-seven."

"Mmmhmm, and you don't have any kids? That includes any that might be on the way." she said, looking right at him.

This time, Luther chuckled. He was next to Mini so he leaned down and kissed her lips.

"Leave this man alone. He answered all of your questions and mine, even the ones you asked more than once."

"Oh my God, you'd think he was asking me to marry him or something," Najah mumbled with an attitude.

"Don't make me cuss you out, little girl. This is my house and I can ask him whatever I want, how many times I want." Mini was speaking to her daughter while she grilled Luther, who laughed at the fact that Mini thought her like or dislike for Gotti was going to affect whether Najah continued to date him.

"It's all good. I don't have anything to hide," Gotti said, offering up a set of pearly whites.

Mini rolled her eyes and walked over to the stove. "Where's Nova? Anybody heard from her yet?"

"She's coming. She asked me to get the twins because she was going to be late, but she just text and said she'd be here in a minute," Najah said, looking down at her phone, grateful that the focus was no longer on her and Gotti.

"Auggie, when are you going to slow your ass down long enough to find a house for Joy?"

Logic looked up at Joy, who shrugged with a grin. This was the downside to Joy and Mini spending so much time together, sidebar conversations about their personal life.

"I'm working on it." He cut his eyes at Joy and then bit down on her shoulder.

"Hey everybody," Nova said as she entered the kitchen, pulling her purse off her shoulder and then dropping it on the kitchen table. She was followed by Nate, who quickly had everyone's attention.

"Who is this?" Mini asked as her eyes moved from the top of Nate's head down to the Jordans on his feet. He was dressed casually in a pair of jeans and a Nike sweatshirt.

Joy and Najah shared a quick glance and grinned, recognizing Nate from the club, before they focused on him again. Neither of them knew that Nova had called herself friendly enough with Nate for him to be standing in Mini's kitchen for family dinner night.

"This is Nate. He's a friend of mine and—"

Mini held her hand up to silence Nova and then looked at Joy. "Do you know him?" she asked with the most serious expression.

"No, why?" Joy asked in confusion.

"Good, then maybe Auggie won't try to shoot him," Mini said like it was nothing, and then looked right back at Nate. "Welcome, baby, make yourself at home. We're glad to have you. Dinner should be ready in a few, and Nova, get that damn purse off my table, little girl."

Everyone in the kitchen exchanged glances and Luther shook his head while Mini continued moving around like she hadn't just said the craziest thing ever. It caused them all to smile, but no one said a word about it. Mini was Mini, and that wasn't changing for anyone.

The rest of dinner went about the same. Mini took shots at everyone because she could, and no one but Luther was going to challenge that, which he did from time to time. Nate seemed to fit right in, which was a relief to Nova, and she was even impressed that Logic and Gotti got along with him. The three spent time with Trent and Kenyan playing the game and having guy talk while the girls chilled and did their own thing.

As the night went on, Luther and Mini disappeared, which didn't go unnoticed, leaving the crew to fend for themselves. Trent and Kenyan were deep into a movie while Kenya slept peacefully next to them, leaving the adults to conversation amongst themselves.

"What the fuck does a corporate lawyer do?" Gotti asked Nate, who was sitting across the room in the La-Z-Boy with Nova on his lap.

Gotti was on one end of the sofa with Najah on his lap, while Logic was stretched out on the other end, one leg across it while the other rested on the floor. Joy was positioned between his legs with his arms around her.

Nate chuckled because he got that a lot. Not many people understood his job. "It's like private legal counsel for the company I work for. I help with contracts and acquisitions, but I guess the easiest way to explain it is I make sure they get their money's worth with every deal they make."

"You like that shit? It sounds boring as fuck," Logic said, which made Nova roll her eyes.

Nate laughed. "It's alright, but you're right, it is boring as fuck. Pays the bills though, so it's whatever."

"I feel you on that. Get that paper anyway you can," Logic said with a grin.

"Absolutely." Nate agreed.

He knew from the time he laid eyes on Gotti and Logic what their profession was. There were subtle clues like the fact the neither of them had actual jobs, but were dressed in expensive attire. Their mannerisms and conversation were also a dead giveaway, which connected the dots on why Nova didn't want him around her family. He didn't really care one way or the other.

Nate wasn't from the streets, but had no issue with anyone who was. How Logic and Gotti lived was none of his business, and he planned to make that clear to Nova so that she would be at ease about him being a part of her life. After tonight, seeing how free and loving she was around her family, he knew that he was slowly falling, and planned to make that clear to her.

"Aight, bet, so when I need to negotiate some deals and acquire some shit, I'm gonna give you a call," Logic said.

"I got you." Nate said and then kissed Nova on the temple.

"Yo, what I want to know is why the fuck your ass didn't get the third degree like I did," Gotti asked, pointing at Nate.

"Because you look shady as fuck, and he's a suit and tie type brother," Logic said.

"No hell, he's rocking jeans and Jays. *YOUR* mother just be on that bullshit," Najah said, making them all laugh.

"Why she gotta be my mother just because she went in on his shady ass."

Najah rolled her eyes and knocked Logic's leg off the sofa.

"Yo, chill, don't be mad. It's all good, Nah Nah. It's just because she loves you more than she loves Nova," Logic teased.

"Oh, hell no, it just means that she trusts my decision making skills more than she trust hers," Nova said, pointing at Najah.

"Do we really wanna go there?" Najah said with a smirk.

"Man, don't bring that shit up before you fuck around and piss me off," Logic said, getting annoyed.

A conversation about Rah was the last thing he wanted right now, and he knew that was where Najah was going with that.

Joy tilted her head back and kissed Logic to calm him down, knowing that him thinking about Rah wasn't good on any level.

"Well, on that note, I think it's time for us to go. It's late and I'm tired." Nova lifted her body from Nate's and he followed, standing behind her and sliding his arm around her waist.

Everyone else followed so that they could say their goodbyes. Nova and Nate got the twins ready to go, and Najah and Gotti did the same with Trent, since the two were staying at his place. After everyone said their goodbyes, Mini and Luther made an appearance before everyone left. Family dinner night had been a success, which everyone was grateful for, but Nova more than anybody. Maybe things were starting to fall into place.

*****

"Stay with me tonight?" Nate said when he pulled up in front of Nova's apartment. The twins were asleep in the back seat of his car and he wasn't quite ready for their evening to end.

"I can't do that. They have school tomorrow." Nova glanced over her shoulder at Kenyan and Kenya, who were both knocked out.

"I'll bring you home in the morning. I don't have to go in until nine."

Nova looked at Nate, who had an intense stare as he waited for her answer. She was so entranced by his looks. His chocolate complexion and dark eyes were sexy to her. Combined with a body that was well worth the time she spent admiring it, she knew she could easily fall for him. He had the sweetest personality, which surfaced anytime he dealt with her and the twins, but he also had a protective side to him, which she'd witnessed firsthand.

While out to eat one night, a random guy got too friendly with her, which rubbed Nate the wrong way. It only took a minute for him to make it very clear that he wasn't to be messed with, and neither was anyone he valued. Nova was now in that category, so needless to say, the guy who approached her quickly backed down and apologized.

"Maybe that's not a good idea."

Nova didn't know how much will power she would have, sleeping in the same bed with Nate. She was more than attracted, and he had no issues letting her know that he felt the same. They had yet to stay the night with together. Although Nate had damn near seen her naked because he wasn't shy about being around her while she dressed or undressed, she didn't know if he would be able to stick to the no sex rule that she had insisted on and still be that close to her all night.

"Why not? You think you'll break down and let me have this?" Nate's hand moved between her legs while a smirk spread across his face.

Nova's body reacted so fast she quickly removed his hand and clenched her thighs together to stop the flow that was happening.

He laughed. "I'll play by your rules. You can even sleep in the guest room with the twins if you want, although I would prefer that you slept in my bed with me. I just want to spend more time with you, so go home with me."

Nova searched his face, already knowing her answer before she let out a sigh. "Fine, let me go get a few things." She looked over her shoulder again.

"I'll stay here with them," Nate offered, pleased that she had given in.

Nova hesitated for a minute before she opened her door and got out. She left to go pack a few things for her and the twins, and an hour later they were at Nate's house. The twins were sleeping peacefully in one of his guest rooms while Nate showered and she walked around his house getting familiar with it.

His house was decent size, nothing over the top, but nice. A lot nicer that what Nova was used to, and it made her feel insecure to be there. She couldn't understand what on earth he was doing with her. Nate clearly had things together and could have anyone he wanted. He was successful, had money, a nice house, was sexy as hell, basically the perfect catch. Nova had looks, there was no question about that, but at this point in her life that was all she could offer.

Standing at his sliding door staring out at his backyard, Nova surveyed her surroundings. The lights from the pool created a warm glow that made her want to jump in it.

"What you thinking about?" Nate's body pressed against Nova's from behind while his arms moved around her waist and his lips grazed the side of her face.

"How come you're single?" she asked.

Nate knew the question was deeper than it appeared, so he turned her to face him and planted a kiss on her lips

"How come I'm single or how come I chose you?"

Nova frowned a little, not liking the fact that she was so readable.

He smiled, took her hand, and led her to the living room where he sat down, pulling her with him. Sitting Indian style, while she waited for his answer.

"I work all the time. In fact, the night I met you, my boy damn near threatened me to go out. I had just finished a deal where I was in the office and meetings for damn near two weeks straight 24/7. It was his birthday, so I agreed. My job takes a lot of time, and the women I usually meet care more about my bottom line than who I am. They have no problem taking, but it's the giving that they struggle with. I'm simple, I want someone honest, who's willing to be themselves no matter what the situation, and are happy just to be with me. That's you. You are who you are. You're not perfect. Hell, neither am I, but we fit, or at least I think so. I like who I am with you."

"I don't need anyone to save me, if that's what you're thinking."

He laughed. "Why the fuck would I need to save you, and from what? You seem very capable of doing whatever is necessary to survive. Do I want to make your life easier? Hell yeah, but that's not about saving you. That's just about me sharing my privileges with you. I work hard for all this, and for what? To sit around and look at it, alone? What's the point if I can't share it with somebody? Be that somebody. It's that simple."

Nova couldn't hide the smile that formed. Yes, Nate was different. She knew that from their first conversation, but sitting there right now and listening to him explain how he felt definitely confirmed that he was exactly what she needed. There were no guarantees, but she was definitely going to give them a chance.

# -13-

"**Y**our ass got some explaining to do," Najah said when she walked through Nova's bedroom door and flopped down on her bed.

"Man, bye, mind your business, Nah Nah." Nova rolled her eyes and continued folding the load of clothes that sat on her bed.

Najah had just finished her last class for the day and had decided to stop by and get the 411 on Nova and Nate. It shocked the hell out of her and everybody else when she showed up with him at their family dinner.

"Hoe, please. Your business is my business, so spill. I shouldn't even have to be here asking you this because it's your job to keep me informed anyway," Najah said after she grabbed one of Nova's towels and threw it at her.

"Did I show up at your house unannounced, digging all into your personal business about Gotti?"

Najah looked at her cousin with a smirk. "No, hoe, you called me and grilled me instead, but I felt like making a house call, so spill."

Nova laughed and gave in. "We're just chillin'. It's nothing major."

"Mmmhmm, if it's nothing major then why was he all up in my mama's house, and why weren't you at yours last night?"

"How do you know I wasn't at home?" Nova's face scrunched up.

"I didn't, but you just told on yourself," Najah said with a sly grin.

"Man, I hate your ass sometimes, I swear." Nova rolled her eyes and lifted the stack of towels she had just folded before heading to the hall closet to put them away. When she returned to her room, she snatched her phone from her cousin's hand and then fell out on her bed. "Damn, you're nosey."

"Well, if you would just tell me what's up, I wouldn't have to be all up in your phone."

"There's nothing to tell. I said we're just chillin'," Nova said, rolling over onto her back and scrolling through her texts with a grin plastered all over her face while she reread their recent conversation.

"Man, are you really going to act like that? Nova, just tell me," Najah whined.

"You're so damn extra. He's cool, I like him."

"And?"

"And what?"

"He's sexy as fuck, Nova. Details girl."

Nova frowned. "There are no details. I'm not going there with him yet. I need to be sure first."

"Damn, Nova. You and Gotti both are getting on my damn nerves. I can't get none from him, so the least you can do is let me live vicariously through you."

Nova burst out laughing. "Damn, Najah, he still holding out on you?"

"Hell yeah. He claims I need to get my head right, but I swear he be on some shit. How you gone have me half naked licking and sucking damn near every inch of my body, but won't let me get the full package?"

"Just take it. I guarantee if you pull that *package* out and sit on it, all that get your mind right stuff will be dead. Just like that."

"Girl, I tried. I swear he has control for days." Najah was damn near pouting.

"Well, I don't. It's killing me, but sex makes me stupid and I don't wanna mess this up, so I'm just chillin' right now," Nova admitted. She really wanted things to work with Nate, and sex confused things.

"So you stayed with him, at his house, in his bed, and you didn't give him any?" Najah looked at Nova like she didn't believe her.

"Yes, I did, and no I didn't. It almost killed me because he was all up under me, all damn night, looking good and smelling even better, but I kept my damn legs tight. He knew he was breaking me, though."

"Girl, you better than me. You doing anything right now?" Najah ask looking down at her nails, which were in desperate need of a manicure.

"Yeah, nothing, and that ain't about to change, so whatever you're about to ask me the answer is no," Nova said.

She had a few hours before she had to pick the twins up from school, and she had no plans to leave her house.

"Nova, please, come go to Lola's with me. I'll even pay for you to get yours done," Najah begged.

Nova rolled her eyes. She was not in the mood to deal with any of the fake, shit talking females that she knew would be up in Lola's. It was the cheapest spot to get a bomb ass manicure. The problem was the fact that it was in their neighborhood, which meant that everybody she and Najah knew would be there and ready to be all up in their business. Especially now, since Logic was back in charge, and all the thirsty chicks looking for a come up would be in their faces trying to find a way to get to him through them. It was annoying as hell, and Nova and Najah both hated it.

"Why we gotta go to Lola's? You know them chicks in there be on some shit, and I'm having a good day. I'm not in the mood to lay hands on anybody." Nova sat up with a frown on her face.

"Girl, bye, you know them hoes ain't stupid enough to come at us like that. Besides, Charmaine is the business and you know it. She be having my shit on point. Come on, Nova, go with me, please. In and out, I promise." Najah jumped up and waited for Nova, who rolled her eyes and grabbed her purse.

"You're paying, so don't get in there acting crazy when it's time to leave."

"Girl, I got you. Let's go."

Najah decided to drive, and when she pulled up in front of Lola's and parked, her good day went tragically wrong. The first thing she noticed was Gotti's car parked right in front of the building with him leaning against it like he didn't have a care in the world. Some trick was standing in front of him, looking like she was in a damn daze.

"You don't know what that's about, so don't go up there acting crazy," Nova said, praying that she wasn't about to have to help her cousin lay this chick out.

"What I know is I sent his ass three texts before we left your house, which he hasn't responded to, but he got time to be up here entertaining that bitch," Najah said, pointing toward where Gotti and his friend were standing.

His back was to them, so he had no idea they were in the parking lot until Najah and Nova made it to where they were. Najah stood on the sidewalk about a foot behind the chick that was standing in front of Gotti who was a little too close to him for her liking. They weren't actually touching, but the hoe was definitely in his personal space.

His eyes fell on Najah but his expression didn't change as he spoke to her like he didn't have some other bitch in his face.

"Hold up, ma, give me a minute," he said to Najah before he focused on the chick in front of him again.

The girl's expression was far from neutral as she mugged Najah hard as hell and then turned to Gotti, pointing a finger over her shoulder toward Najah, but keeping her eyes on him.

"Who the fuck is that?" she asked with an undeniable attitude that rubbed Najah the wrong way.

She was seconds away from addressing her, but rethought her decision when Gotti gave her a look that dared her to. She bit the inside of her mouth, remembering the conversation they had about her being able to handle certain situations. When she had agreed, she had no idea how hard it would be to actually keep her mouth shut.

Nova looked at Gotti and the chick first and then Najah, confused about why her cousin was so calm because it was totally out of character for her.

"Nick, don't make me embarrass you out here. She is none of your damn business. Did you hear anything I just told your ass? There ain't shit between me and you anymore, so don't stand here acting like you have the right to question me about who the fuck my girl is."

"Your girl?" Nick turned and eyed Najah, searching her body from head to toe with a scowl on her face. "Since when do you have a girl? I thought you didn't do commitment."

Najah's foot was tapping and she had her jaw clenched to keep from saying anything, but it was damn near killing her.

Nova was amused by the whole situation.

"I never said that, what I said was I wasn't wifing your ass." Gotti pointed at Nick before he pulled a freshly rolled blunt from behind his ear.

He kept his eyes on Najah, knowing that it was taking every ounce of control she had not to say something. He really wanted to laugh at her, but he kept it cool. Nick wasn't anybody important. In fact, she was the last of his females that he was cutting things off with so that he could lock shit down with Najah. The fact that she just happened to roll up on him while he was doing it was inconvenient, but it didn't move him one way or the other.

"You know what? Fuck you, Gotti. You dealing with little kids anyway." She glanced at Najah. "So I don't need this shit."

Gotti lit his blunt and looked right at Najah, knowing that she wanted to lay hands on Nick, but she kept her cool, which is exactly what he wanted. He couldn't have any female he was serious about in the streets on some ratchet shit. Besides, she didn't have a damn thing to worry about, and he would make sure she knew that.

He waved his hand in the air, dismissing Nick. "The fuck you still standing here for then?"

Gotti stepped away from his car and grabbed Najah around the waist, leaned down and kissed her while Nick grilled both of them and then stormed off.

"Yo, what up, Nova?" Gotti glanced at her and then looked down at Najah.

"Your little ass is about to explode," he said with a cocky grin.

Najah rolled her eyes.

"I'm going inside so you guys can talk," Nova said.

He looked up and searched the parking lot. When he noticed Najah's car, he looked down at her again. "Yo, give her your keys. Come take a ride with me."

"No, I need to get my nails done." Najah rolled her eyes at him and held her hand up for him to see.

"And she has to pay for mine," Nova added.

Gotti let out a frustrated sigh. "Man, I'll bring your ass back later to get that shit done." He reached in his pocket, pulled out a fold of cash and pulled off a few bills, which he extended to Nova. She gladly accepted.

"'Preciate it," she said with a grin.

"Give her your damn keys," he said, looking at Najah again.

Nova snatched the keys from her before she had a chance to object, and Najah rolled her eyes at both them.

"Bye, cuz," Nova said over her shoulder as she headed to the door.

Gotti took Najah's hand in his and damn near dragged her to his car. He opened the passenger side door and she sucked her teeth before falling into the seat. He chuckled because he knew she was mad, but she didn't really have a reason to be. Instead of addressing it, he decided to let her have her moment.

Najah pouted the entire drive to his apartment, but Gotti kept his thoughts about it to himself until he parked and turned the car off.

"I don't know what you sitting there looking crazy for," he said with a grin that pissed Najah off even more.

She gave him the nastiest look before folding her arms across her chest. "Why are we here?"

He chuckled. "Because we need to talk. Now come on."

Gotti opened his door and got out, but Najah didn't move. She took a deep breath and let it out slowly, trying her best not to tell him what she was really thinking. When Gotti realized she wasn't moving, he walked to her door and opened it for her. After resting his arm on the roof, he leaned down and looked at her.

"Would you come on? I'm really not in the mood."

Najah looked up at him like he was crazy. "Not in the mood?" She sucked her teeth. "Maybe I wasn't in the mood to see you with some trick in your face."

Gotti smiled and grabbed her arm, forcing her out the car. She didn't resist, so it really didn't take much effort. He hit the locks and then used his key to get in his apartment, shutting and locking the door behind him. Najah stood in the center of the living room with her arms folded across her chest while he was on his way to his bedroom, not really moved by the fact that she wasn't behind him.

Najah stood there for a minute, waiting for what, she didn't know. Eventually, she gave in and made her way to his bedroom, where she found him sitting on the foot of his bed facing the door, waiting with a grin on his face.

"Well?" Najah asked from the door where she had stopped and stood.

Gotti laughed at how petty she was being. He thought her little attitude was cute.

"What you mad for?"

"Because—"

"Because you rolled up on me unannounced, while I was cutting shit off with someone who is totally irrelevant to you or me." He stopped her from talking before she had a chance to say something crazy.

"Who was that?" Najah asked, feeling silly because he was right, and she didn't know what else to say.

"My past. Now do you want to stand there questioning me about shit that don't matter, or you wanna come join me?"

"Is she the only one?" Najah asked.

Gotti smiled. "You know the answer to that, but the bigger question is, did I disrespect you in any way or did I make it clear that *YOU* were my priority?" He pointed at her.

Najah tried to hold in her smile, but it was forcing its way through anyway.

"The fuck you smiling for now? You had your ass on your shoulders for the last twenty minutes over some bullshit." Gotti looked at her with a cocky smirk.

"At least I didn't put my hands on that hoe, like I really wanted to," Najah said, which made him chuckle.

"You better be glad you didn't, or you wouldn't be here right now. I told you I don't play that shit. You don't need to put your hands on somebody over me, ever. If it's some shit I need to handle, I will, and I will never let anyone be disrespectful to you, but you have to trust me on that. I appreciate you trusting me on that today, so stop being stubborn so I can show you just how much I appreciate it."

Najah stood there grinning, but finally gave in and made her way over to him. She stood between his legs while he looked up at her, not moving for a minute, just holding a stare with her.

"You with me, Najah?" Gotti asked as he pulled her shirt over her head and then tossed it across the room.

She bit her bottom lip and nodded.

"You ready for this?" he asked, sliding his hand into her leggings while he kept his eyes on her.

Again, she nodded.

"You better be, because there's no turning back."

Najah leaned in and kissed him to further confirm that she had no doubts. She had been waiting and wasn't about to back down, so she stepped out of her Nikes while Gotti worked her leggings down her body.

He was about to make things official in a way that would wipe out any doubts that she could possibly have.

# -14-

"**W**ould you quit looking at me like that?" Joy asked, grinning at Logic who was across from her on his sofa. She had her iPad in her hands, swiping through photos of yet another house she wanted to check out. They had three lined up to see the next day, and she still couldn't stop looking.

Logic's eyes traced Joy's body as he started calculating in his head. He was trying to remember the last time that Joy had her period, and kept coming back to the same thing. The week after they visited his lake house. That was almost a month and a half ago, so she had to be pregnant. He scrunched up his face, trying to decide if she knew and wasn't telling him or if she hadn't really paid much attention to it.

There had been so much going on in their lives lately that it would have been easy to miss. In fact, the only reason he thought about it was because he noticed subtle changes in her body. He knew every inch of her body, how it looked and how it felt, so simple things stood out, like the way her breasts were filling out, and the fact that the last few times he had slid up in her, she had damn near drowned him, she was so wet. She would come home every day drained and dying to take a nap, which he thought was about her staying up late with him, but now he wasn't so sure. Something was different, and the only thing he could think of was that she was that she was pregnant. Had to be.

"What about this one?" Joy crawled over to him, positioning her body between his legs before holding up her iPad and showing him pictures of the house that she had been looking at. His mind was still stuck on her being pregnant, so he just nodded, which annoyed her.

"Never mind." She tried to sit up, but he pulled her back into his body and kissed her neck.

"Chill, Joy, with your stubborn ass, damn. I like it. We can try to see that one tomorrow too, if you want. But right now, get your ass up so we can go to bed."

It was already after midnight, and Joy knew she had to be up at six to make it to work by seven, but lately, since Logic had been gone so much, she had tried her best to stay up with him whenever he was home. Because of the hours he had been keeping, his system had quickly adjusted to being up late, so it didn't faze him, but he could tell that it was messing with Joy. If she was up late with him, she was dead tired by the time she got home from work, and usually asleep within minutes of hitting the front door. But now he had something else in mind as to what was causing her to sleep so much.

"Are you coming?" she asked with a slight pout.

Logic wasn't tired, but he knew that she wanted him in bed with her, so he agreed.

"Yeah, come on, I got you."

He waited for her to stand, and then followed. They made their way to the bedroom and Joy snuggled close to him, wrapping her body around his. All he could think was that this shit right here was life. No matter what was going on in his world, Joy close to him, her skin against his skin, was everything.

Logic lay awake long after Joy was asleep, trying to figure out his next move. It had been heavy on his mind for the past couple weeks, but with all the chaos that had surrounded them, he hadn't really had a chance to slow down enough to figure out what he wanted to do. Buying a house was one thing, but he really wanted more. He wanted to make things permanent, and the possibility of Joy being pregnant had really brought things full circle. Now it was just a matter of him bringing it all together, and that was exactly what he planned to do.

He tightened his hold on Joy and kissed the top of her head before closing his eyes and trying to settle his mind enough to go to sleep, but Logic knew that was wishful thinking. His mind was working overtime processing his plans, so he prepared himself for a long night with no sleep.

The next morning, he woke up to the sound of Joy moving around the room. He had no idea when he had actually fallen asleep, but it hadn't been that long ago. Logic grinned as he watched Joy trying her best to stay quiet, but the space was so small that she was failing miserably. She was so stuck in her rush to get ready that she hadn't even noticed he was up and watching her until his voice startled her.

"Why you so damn loud, Joy?" Logic had rolled over onto his back and folded one arm behind his head while the other rested on his bare chest.

She frowned and walked over to him. After leaning down for a peck on the lips, she offered up a quick apology and then tried to pull away. "Sorry."

Logic's hand gripped her waist and pulled her toward him, causing Joy to fall onto his body.

"You're late," he said and kissed her neck a few times before she freed herself from him and moved to the closet.

"I know. I didn't hear my alarm." Again, she frowned as she stepped into a pair of khaki slacks and zipped them.

Logic watched her with a grin, admiring her body, mostly her breasts until she pulled on a silk button up blouse and covered them with it. She worked her fingers down the buttons before she shoved the hem into her pants and then pulled it out just a little.

"Are you meeting me at the school, or should I meet you here?" she asked as she spun on her heels to face the dresser, yanking her hair out of the ponytail that it was in and then grabbing a comb and running it through her hair.

"I'll meet you there." Logic tossed the covers back and stood.

After a full stretch, he walked up behind Joy and kissed her on the cheek before leaving the room. His mind was on his day. He had a lot to get done while she was at work.

*****

"Aye, I'm looking for Karma, can you tell me where to find her?"

The receptionist looked Logic over and smiled lustfully. "And who may I tell her is asking?" she said, lifting the phone's receiver from its base and grinning at him.

"Logic," he said dryly, hoping that she would get the picture.

"Damn, that's sexy, just like you. It fits." She dialed a number and then began to speak, so he waited and listened.

"Ms. Jackson, there's a Logic here to see you. Should... Oh, okay. I'll send him back." She looked up at him and rolled her eyes before she addressed Logic again. "Back that way, second office on the left," she rattled off, pointing over her shoulder without even looking at him.

He shrugged and followed her instructions. When he reached Karma's office he stepped inside. She smiled, walked around her desk and offered him a friendly hug before sitting down behind it again and pointing to a chair in front of her desk for him.

"Yo, what did you say to old girl out there? She looked like she wanted to cuss me out after she hung up," Logic said and then sat down in front of Karma and leaned back in his chair.

Karma sucked her teeth. "I told her thirsty ass if she even looked at you a second time, I was gonna beat her ass."

Logic laughed. "Damn, why you do it like that? She wasn't worried about me."

"Man, please, her thirsty ass already had your first born named the second you entered the building."

"Yo, you tripping." Logic chuckled because he could tell Karma was serious and she wasn't backing down.

"Joy send you here? What's up, y'all good?"

"Nah, she don't know I'm here, so I would appreciate it if you didn't tell her."

Karma sat up and gave him a funny look. She didn't keep secrets from Joy, and wasn't about to start. Especially if they involved her man, which this one clearly did since he was there. She liked Logic, but she loved Joy, who was basically her sister.

"Man, fix your damn face. I need help with something." Logic grinned, reading into Karma's expression.

"Help with what? And if Joy didn't send you here then how the hell did you know where I worked? I damn sure didn't tell you." Karma peered at him.

"Joy mentioned it one day, but I didn't know how to find it, so I looked it up. Harbor has like three damn locations down here, and of course you worked at the last one I checked," Logic said in frustration, remembering the past hour he'd spent trying to find Karma.

He didn't know her last name, and all he knew was that she worked for Harbor, which he Googled and found out was an ad agency with three divisions. He had to go to each one looking like a damn stalker asking about her because he really didn't know shit about Karma other than she was Joy's best friend.

Karma laughed. "So you walked up in there asking about me? What did they say."

"The first place damn near called security because I didn't know your last name, and at the second place, the one on Edge Drive, a shorty felt sorry for me and told me where to find you. Got me looking like a stalker and shit, real talk, yo."

Karma smiled and leaned back again. "So what was so important that you had to find me and not tell Joy?"

"I need you to help me find her a ring."

Karma's eye bucked. "A ring, ring, like as in I do, ring?" She was grinning from ear to ear.

"Yeah, damn. Why you all excited and shit like it's for you?" Logic teased at Karma's excitement.

"Because that's my girl and I'm happy." Karma rolled her eyes.

"So can you help me? Like take lunch or something to help me pick one. I figured if anybody will know what she likes, you would."

"Hell yeah, I know," Karma insisted.

"Don't be picking shit you want. This is for Joy, and I need it to be perfect." Logic pointed at Karma, grilling her just a little.

"Man, shut up, I got this. Hang on." She lifted her phone and made a call.

"I'm going to lunch early and I should be back in a few hours. I'm putting my phone on do not disturb so that it will go straight to voicemail. Can I have my business, damn?" Karma said and then hung up.

Logic shook his head, laughing to himself at how different she and Joy were. He waited while Karma opened her drawer, lifted her purse out of it and then stood.

"Aight, let's do this," she said with a grin.

She led the way, with Logic right behind her.

When they passed the receptionist, she spoke up. "Have fun, I'll be sure to let Lan know if he comes by looking for you."

Karma held her hand up and shot her a bird, which made Logic laugh.

"Y'all tight, I see," he said just before he opened the passenger side door to let Karma into his car.

Once he was in the driver's seat, she dropped her purse on the floor. "She's nosey as fuck, and seconds away from me putting my foot in her ass is what we are."

Logic chuckled and headed to the mall.

After three stores and what felt like a hundred rings, Logic had finally purchased what satisfied him as the perfect choice for Joy. A princess cut diamond set in a platinum band. Karma was so excited that she could barely contain it, and had damn near planned out everything from the proposal through her vision of their wedding. Logic didn't understand how women got so caught up in stuff like that, but clearly it was a big deal.

"Yo, let's catch lunch. It's the least I can do since you wasted your lunch helping me with this shit."

"This is not shit. This is the absolute best surprise ever, but you can still feed me." Karma held up the bag that the ring was in, which she had insisted on guarding with her life.

"Aight, you choose. I'm good with anything."

Karma looked around and then decided on Chili's since it was just across the street. Logic drove through the parking lot of the mall and made his way to Chili's. After he parked, the two of them got out again, with Karma holding onto the ring for dear life.

"You know I can put that in the trunk," Logic said, pointing to the bag.

"No hell, you are such a man, I swear. I know you can probably afford to buy ten more, but this one is perfect and needs to be kept in sight at all times. I don't have the energy to go through that again." She rolled her eyes and waited while he opened the door and let her enter. He followed and they waited for a hostess to seat them.

Once they were at their table, Karma lifted her menu and began surveying it, but was quickly snapped out of her thoughts when she heard a familiar voice behind her.

"Who the fuck is that, K?"

Karma looked up just in time to see Lan grilling Logic hard as hell. In all the months that Joy had been with him, Landon had never actually seen Joy and Logic together.

"Landon, I'm going to our table."

Karma's expression turned hard the second she laid eyes on Lexus, who grinned at her as she placed her hand on Landon's arm. He turned to her and knocked her hand off his arm before turning to Karma and Logic again.

"This is none of your business, but apparently that is." Karma said, pointing to Lexus as Landon's eyes hit the bag that held Joy's ring and he got heated.

Logic followed his eyes, noticed his expression change, and didn't want things to get worse. So he offered a hand. "Logic, me and Joy—"

"The fuck you doing here with Joy's man with jewelry bags and shit. Is this some kind of date or something?"

"Why the fuck are you here with her while she's putting her hands on you, is that some kind of date?"

"He's my producer, why wouldn't we have lunch together? We do all the time."

"Look, bruh, you can calm that shit down. This ain't a fucking date, this is just a thank you because she helped me pick an engagement ring for Joy." Logic was now on his feet squared up, and speaking to Landon in a way that dared him to say something else disrespectful.

"I'll let you deal with her, I'll be at our table." Lexus touched Landon's arm again, which caused Karma to jump up.

"Yo, why the fuck you keep doing that shit? You know better than to put your hands on me, and we, as in you and me, don't have lunch together. This is a business fucking meeting with Ross, so chill with that shit. And if you put your damn hands on me one more time you'll be finding another producer and another fucking beat for your new song." Landon pointed at Lexus who stood there looking stupid as a Ross walked up.

"What's up, Karma," he said cheerfully until he surveyed the situation and realized that everyone was tense.

"Yo, take her dumb ass to the car. I done lost my fucking appetite. We can do this shit at the studio," Landon said, waving his hand at Ross before he turned to Logic. "My bad, bruh, you have to appreciate how this shit looks, but we're good."

Logic eyed Landon but accepted the hand he had extended toward him. "We're good. I'll give you guys a minute," Logic said and stepped around them to head to the bathroom.

"Why do you keep dealing with her if you know she wants you like that?" Karma asked the second Logic was gone.

"We're not doing this again. You know why, K. She just got her deal, her single is weeks away from hitting the air, and I need that exposure. I don't want that damn girl. When the hell you gonna start believing what I say? That shit right there is just business. That's it. She can shit in one hand and put her wants in the other and see which one fills up first. Ain't nothing happening."

"That's just hard for me to believe, and that's your fault."

"Man, you need to pick a side. I know I fucked up a lot, but that was then and this is now. You can't say you want shit to work in one breath, and then follow it up with you don't trust me with the next. It don't work like that, K."

Karma stood there not saying anything because she knew he was right, but it didn't change that fact that she had trust issues and it was his fault. When Karma didn't speak, he grabbed her around the waist and placed his lips against hers for a quick kiss.

"I'm not perfect, K, but I'm trying. I'm not fucking around. You have to believe that. I need you to believe that. I can't be out here making moves if I'm constantly stressing about what you think. I don't want that damn girl or any other for that matter. It's you and me, okay? I need you to believe that. I made it hard for you to do so, but just promise me you'll try. I got you and only you. I put my life on that."

Karma rolled her eyes as a smile broke through. She loved Landon and couldn't deny that, and she trusted him the best she could. But when things like this happened it was easy to doubt.

"Fine, but if she comes for me one more time, she's gonna need plastic surgery to fix her damn face before they shoot her album cover. Now try me."

Just as she said that, Logic walked up and chuckled, hearing what Karma said. He sat down since they were standing a few feet away from their table, but Landon released Karma, dropped one arm around her shoulder and turned to him.

"Yo, my bad about all that, and I really hope we're straight. I just don't play about this one," Landon said.

Logic chuckled. "Nah, you good. I get it. I don't know what you got going on, but you can join us if you want."

Landon let out a frustrated breath. "Nah, let me go handle this dumb ass girl before she fucks around and makes me catch a case."

"Yeah, you do that, before I do," Karma said. "In fact, let me go—"

"Oh hell no, I got this. Chill, and I'll see you when I get home."

Karma and Landon shared another kiss before he left and then she and Logic settled in for lunch.

# -15-

"**Ma**, where you at?" Logic said, walking into his mother's house and slamming the door behind him without really thinking about it.

He laughed at himself, feeling dumb as he set Joy's ring down on the coffee table in the living room. He had planned to leave it in the car, but for some reason he kept hearing Karma's voice in his head, like she was secretly fussing at him, and ended up taking it with him.

"Why the hell you slamming my door like you don't have no damn sense?" Mini said over her shoulder as soon as she heard Logic behind her. He made his way to her and leaned down enough to wrap his arms around her and then kiss her cheek.

"My bad, I didn't mean to."

"Well, I'm gonna mean to make you pay for it when you knock it off the hinges." She shrugged him off her body and he chuckled then made his way to the table and sat down.

"You hungry?" she asked, turning to face him.

"Nah, I'm good."

"What you want then?" Mini asked as she took a seat in the chair across the table from her son.

"Damn, I can't just come see you. It's like that? Maybe I just wanted to come check you out and see if you're good."

"You can come see me anytime you want, but you don't, unless you want something. So just tell me what it is and quit pretending like you're concerned about my wellbeing."

Logic leaned back in his chair and grinned at the serious expression his mother wore.

"I need to run something by you."

"I'm listening." Mini leaned back and folded her arms across her chest.

"Hang on."

Logic jumped up and went back to the living room where he left Joy's ring. Once he had it, he walked back into the kitchen and placed the tiny bag down in front of his mother before sitting again. She eyed it, looked up at him before reaching inside and pulling out the box that held Joy's ring. After she opened and inspected the ring, she closed it and set it down in front of her.

"When is she due?"

Logic laughed. "There you go, why she gotta be pregnant because I bought her a ring?"

"I'm not saying she's pregnant because you bought her a ring. I'm saying she's pregnant because I could see it all over her the other night at dinner."

Logic waved his mother off and laughed again. "Man, you didn't see shit."

Mini just stared at her son but didn't say a word.

"Man, what? Why you looking at me like that?" he said with a grin.

"Look, little boy, I might be old, but I ain't dead. The same way I knew when Najah and Nova walked their fast asses up in my house pregnant, I knew when Joy did. So you might be in denial and maybe she is too, but she's pregnant, Auggie."

"She doesn't know, or at least I don't think she knows. She hasn't said shit to me about it," Logic admitted, thinking out loud.

When he focused on his mother again, she looked concerned. "What do you mean she doesn't know? How do you know if she doesn't?"

I can just tell, I know her bo... I can just tell." Logic cleaned up his sentence, not wanting to go into detail about how he knew.

Mini laughed and rolled her eyes. "If you think she's pregnant, then I know you're having sex. Hell, it's no damn secret, little boy. You're grown."

"Man, I don't care how grown I am. I don't want you in my business, the same way I don't want to know what you and Luther be doing. That don't work for me."

Again, Mini laughed. "So you bought a ring, what do you need me for? You obviously know what you want to do."

"But that's just it. I don't want her to think I got that because she might be pregnant." Logic pointed to the bag.

"Did you?"

"Did I what?"

"Buy it because she might be pregnant."

"Hell no, I did it because it's what I want. It don't have anything to do with her being pregnant. I just know how y'all get all bent out of shape about that type of stuff."

"You just met her, Auggie. It's only been a little while, so baby or not, you don't have to marry her."

"You know what, never mind. I got it." He was frustrated because he felt like his mom was about to be on some bullshit, and that wasn't what he needed to hear.

"Don't make me slap you, Auggie. Sit down." Mini didn't move, but she spoke with authority and pointed to the chair he was just in.

Logic stared her down for a minute before sitting again.

"Look, I know you love her. Hell, she loves you. No denying that. She made that very clear." Mini smiled, thinking about how Joy had gone toe to toe with her about her son. "But what I don't want is for you to make a quick choice that's influenced by circumstances. I did that with your father and look where it got me."

"Man, fuck him. Don't even bring that shit up. I'm not Hoover, and the situations are not the damn same."

"Keep cussing me, Auggie," Mini threatened. "I'm not saying that you're him. Aside from his blood, you didn't get a damn thing from him. What I'm saying is I married your father because I was pregnant, and I thought that would change things. I thought that he would respect me more and let me get off the streets. I know the situations are different, Auggie. Joy ain't me, but I still married Hoover because I was pregnant with you. I don't want you to make that choice for her. If you want this because it's really where you heart is then I support you a hundred percent. Just be sure, is all I'm saying."

Logic nodded before he got up and kissed his mother on the cheek. He lifted the ring, placed it in the bag and Mini stood.

"I'm out. We have to go check on a few houses today, so I'll catch up with you later."

Logic led the way and Mini followed as they headed to the door.

"I love you, Auggie. You know that, don't you?"

He grinned. "Sometimes," he teased before hugging her and then opening the door. He stepped through it and then turned to wink at her.

The second he turned his back, Mini yelled behind him, "And make that slow ass girl take a damn pregnancy test. How the hell you don't know if you're pregnant? I swear," Mini said and rolled her eyes before shutting the door.

Logic just shook his head and got in his car.

*****

"Excuse me." Logic was standing in front of two shelves of pregnancy tests confused as hell. His arms were folded when he wasn't massaging his temple, so when the lady who worked there walked by him he decided to ask for help.

"Yes?" She stopped next to him and looked up with a smile.

"I need one of these, and *I* don't know what to buy? Well, I don't need one, but, shit, you know what I mean."

She laughed. "Well, they all pretty much do the same thing. Some are just fancier than others."

"Why the hell they make so many, then? Damn," he said. "What would you chose?"

She lifted two boxes from the shelf and handed them to him. "Try these."

He looked down at the boxes, took the two from her hands, and then grabbed one more of each so that he could have two of each one.

She laughed at him. "Can I help you with anything else?"

"Nope, I'm good, I think this got it. 'Preciate it," Logic said as he left the aisle heading to the register.

After he paid, he tossed the tests in the trunk and then left the store parking lot to meet Joy at her school. The realtor had already called and was waiting for them at the first house they were scheduled to see, but at this point, Logic had pregnancy tests and engagement rings on his mind. He had to focus long enough to get through the houses they were viewing and then after that figure out how to get Joy to take the test without cussing him out.

Two hours later, they were at the last house and Joy stood in the center of the massive living room grinning. She was excited about all of the houses they had viewed, pretty much to the point where Logic couldn't really tell which one she liked the most, until now.

"What do you think, Joy?" Melinda looked right at her after a quick glance at Logic. "This one is absolutely gorgeous, isn't it?"

Joy looked at Logic, as if waiting for him to respond, until he laughed, and pointed at Melinda, their real estate agent.

Hell, they hadn't asked him a damn thing the entire time they did their walk through, so there was no need to start now. It was Joy, what do you think of this, and Joy, do you love the colors? Logic could see now that his vote was irrelevant, but he was cool with that. If Joy liked it, then he loved it.

"This place is perfect. I just don't even know what else to say about it."

"Well, Logic, I guess we have a winner," Melinda said, clasping her hands together and then smiling at him.

She saw dollar signs. He was paying cash, and this house was the most expensive of the four that they had viewed. Forty-eight hundred square feet, two car garage, swimming pool, five bedrooms, wood and tile floors and brand new stainless steel appliances. They had just finished construction on this house a month ago, and it would be one of two that would be tucked away on a private street in a gated community. That was the part that Logic liked most. Privacy, and hardly no neighbors. Joy liked the house because it was pretty.

"Looks that way," Logic said, catching Joy's hand and bringing her to him.

After planting a few kisses on her cheek and then lips, their eyes connected. "Is this what you want?"

Melinda cleared her throat. "I'm going to head outside and make a few calls so that you two can discuss it." She offered a smile before heading toward the front door.

"Well?" Logic asked, waiting for Joy's reply.

"I do, but it's a lot of money."

Logic chuckled. "Yeah, it is, but I knew that before we got here. If I wasn't considering it, then I wouldn't have let you fall in love with it. I don't care how much it cost. If you want it, it's yours."

"Are you sure? It's really a lot of money," Joy said with a grin.

"Which you already know I have. Nothing is too much for you. I don't spend money on dumb shit, so this makes sense. Let me worry about the price tag, you just worry about filling up those damn bedrooms." Logic kissed Joy again and waited for her to respond.

"I want it," she said after placing her lips against his.

"Okay, then, looks like we have a house. Now let's go, we have something to take care of."

"What?" Joy asked with a slight frown.

"Just come on."

The two met Melinda outside and settled up on plans to meet her in a few days to finalize the paperwork for the sale of the house. After all the arrangements were made, they swung by Joy's school to get her car, and then she followed Logic back to his apartment.

When they got there, she immediately stripped out of her clothes and headed straight to the bathroom to shower while Logic made a trip to his car to get the pregnancy test and the ring. He set the test on the kitchen counter while removing the ring from the box and sliding it into his pocket before he got comfortable and waited for Joy to finish her shower. The second he laid eyes on her he hopped up.

"Sit down, I need to talk to you about something?"

Joy frowned, but did as instructed, keeping her eyes on him as he sat down in front of her on the coffee table that was across from the sofa she was on.

"What's wrong?" Joy asked, looking concerned.

Logic chuckled. "Nothing's wrong, in fact, shit couldn't get any better than this."

"Then what do you need to talk to me about?" Joy asked, still not convinced.

"You love me?" Logic asked with the most serious expression that made Joy even more nervous. He kept saying nothing was wrong, but his mood was making her extremely nervous.

"You know I do, why?"

"Because this right here is life to me. I don't think I could survive with it being any other way. I swear on everything, you make everything in my life make sense. I know who I am and what I do complicates things, but Joy, I love you with everything in me. I don't even know how to say it other than we make sense. You and me, we just make sense, and I want that forever."

"So do I," Joy said.

"You mean that?" Logic asked with a cocky grin.

"Yeah, of course I do."

"Then prove it."

Joy searched his face. She had no idea what he meant by that. "How?"

"Say yes?"

"Yes to what?"

Logic leaned back and reached in his pocket.

It was all starting to make sense to Joy now, and her hand flew over her mouth. Before he could even get the ring out of his pocket, she was on her feet with her arms around his neck. "Are you serious? Hell yes!"

She held him so tight that he had to pry her arms away just to get the ring out of his pocket.

"Damn, I wasted my money on this shit. You already said yes before I even gave it to you. I might as well take it back to the store."

Joy balled up her fist and nailed him in the shoulder. "Shut up, let me see it."

"Nah, too late. I'm taking this shit back."

"Then I renig too."

Joy held her hand out and waited. Logic laughed and slid the ring on her finger and Joy's face lit up.

"Well?" he asked after a few minutes of Joy grinning and observing the ring.

"I love it." Joy threw her arms around his neck and kissed him. "How did you do this?"

"Karma," Logic said as he pulled away from Joy and walked to the counter to get the bag that the tests were in.

"Karma?" Joy repeated.

"Yep, long story, but I asked her to help me. She did and you love it, so mission accomplished."

Joy grinned, thinking about the two people she loved the most, creating one of the happiest moments in her life. "I have to go call her. I know she's waiting. Did you tell her when you were doing it?"

"No, and you can call her later, this first."

Joy frowned at the bag he was holding "What's this?" Joy opened the bag and then her expression really dropped.

"Umm, why did you buy me pregnancy tests? Do you think I'm pregnant? I'm not pregnant, Logic. Is that why you did this?"

"Man, no. I knew you were going to think that shit. That," he pointed at her hand, "has nothing to do with this, and I already know you're pregnant. I just need for you to know, so let's go."

He grabbed Joy's hand and started walking toward the hall. She yanked away and stopped.

"What do you mean, you know I'm pregnant? I'm not pregnant, Logic. I just had my period..."

Joy paused and started thinking, so Logic finished for her. "The week after we left the lake house and that was damn near two months ago. You haven't had one since then, trust me. As much as I've been up in your shit, I know."

He watched her face while she tried to connect the dots. When the realization hit, she frowned. "Okay, fine, but I'm not pregnant."

Joy snatched the bag from his hand and headed toward the bathroom with Logic right behind her. Before he could enter, she slammed the door. He leaned against the wall and chuckled. *Yeah, your emotional ass is pregnant,* he thought as he prepared to wait.

# -16-

"**A**uggie, get those damn kids before I snatch both of them up," Mini yelled with one hand on her hip and the other pointing toward Logic Jr. and Leia.

Logic grinned because he had been watching them for the past fifteen minutes knowing they were driving his mother crazy. He honestly didn't think she would last this long with the two of them racing back and forth through the kitchen chasing each other, while she was trying to finish up the last of the sides for the dinner that they were having. Since Logic and Joy had the most space, whenever they had a family function it was held at their house. They didn't really mind though, and in fact they enjoyed it. In the past two years there had been so many birthdays, family dinner nights and holidays celebrated in their home that it just didn't feel right to have it any other way.

This day was no different. The house was full, kids had been running in and out all day, but thankfully, Kenyan was playing with her iPad and Kenyan and Trent were in the back yard. Otherwise, Logic knew for sure that his mother would lose it. She loved her grandkids, but not when she had all of them in one house at the same time. Especially not right now, since his two-year-old twins, who seemed to think that they were running the show, were tearing through the house like wild animals.

"I got them," Joy said as she entered through the back door.

She quickly scooped Leia up in her arms and grabbed LJ by the hand, guiding them toward their playroom. Logic watched her as she moved through the house with their children and smiled. That was an image that never got old to him and he knew that he could spend the rest of his life just being around the three of them and never complain.

"Y'all got those damn kids spoiled. They just don't listen to me at all," Mini mumbled before she turned to finish mixing the contents of the bowl that was in front of her.

Logic laughed before he glanced at Luther, who was sitting across from him focused on the game he was watching.

"You need to go handle her with that bad ass attitude."

"You know I can't do anything with her." Luther glanced back at Mini and shook his head.

Logic chuckled. "Yeah, I know, I'm 'bout to head out here and see what's up with Nate and Gotti. You good?"

Luther kept his eyes on the TV, held up the beer he was holding, and nodded, which Logic took to mean that he was good. He left him there in the living room and made his way through the kitchen to the back yard. After a quick stop to kiss his mom and grab a beer, he stepped through the back door where everyone else was.

"Yo, Trent is bad as hell out there. That shit is natural to him," Gotti said the second he laid eyes on Logic.

Trent and Kenyan were both on the court that sat in the corner of their backyard playing around. Logic watched as his nephew stood damn near at what would be considered half court and nailed two threes in a row with no effort.

"He needs to be. He's tall as fuck, yo."

Gotti laughed. "Word, the damn coach made us bring his birth certificate when we signed him up for rec ball. Said there was no way he was eight years old."

"Damn, it's like that?"

"Hell yeah, just like that, and Trent be killing 'em too. They can't do shit with him, real talk."

Najah looked up and rolled her eyes. "You need to stop acting a fool in there before they ban you from his games. You should see him, Auggie, in there at practice taking over for the damn coach like it's his team. They hate to see you coming. Thank God this is a girl," she said and rubbed her stomach, which made Gotti laugh.

"Man fuck that, she might be a baller too."

That really made Najah roll her eyes.

"I still owe your ass an ass whooping for that shit too." Logic pointed to his sister's round belly and Gotti burst out laughing.

"Damn man, I waited two years. The fuck, yo."

"I don't give a fuck, I told you not to get my sister pregnant and I meant that shit."

"Man kiss my ass. We grown."

"Dad, come play?" Trent yelled, holding the ball under one arm and facing the deck that they were all standing on.

Gotti smiled at the fact that Trent had made the decision to call him dad. A grin formed as he thought about the night that Trent came in and sat down next to him on the sofa, looked at him with the most serious expression before saying that he needed to have a man to man with him. Gotti laughed and agreed. When Trent asked him if he could call him dad since his baby sister was going to call him dad, Gotti was floored.

Trent said it was about his baby sister, but Gotti knew better. The two of them had gotten close since he and Najah had been together, and Gotti had made it his business to be a father to Trent. For Gotti, the reason that Trent gave him for wanting to call him dad wasn't important. If Trent was accepting him as his father, then that was what it was gonna be.

"Hang on, I'm coming." Gotti stood, kissed Najah, who was sitting in a chair next to him and rubbed her stomach before leaning down to kiss it.

"You know he's about to embarrass you, right?" Logic said and chuckled.

"I'll redeem myself later with some 2K, just don't record this shit." Gotti said over his shoulder as he took the stairs two at time to join Trent.

"He's that good?' Nate asked, nodding toward the court where Trent was.

"Hell yeah. That shit is crazy. I guess his bitch ass bio, did one thing right. Hell, that's the only thing he did right," Logic said.

Najah held her head back and scrunched up her face to look at her brother. "Don't even mention him. That's MY child and that's his father." She pointed to Gotti, who was now on the court with Trent. Kenyan was sitting on his basketball, on the side now watching the two of them play.

"Your children are about to drive your mother crazy," Joy said when she stepped out the back door and made her way over to Logic. He was leaning against the rail that surrounded the deck, so she positioned her body between his legs before connecting their lips and then turning so that her back was against his chest. Logic's arms moved around her waist and stopped once his hands were resting on her stomach.

"Why they gotta be my kids when they're doing bad shit?" Logic asked with a grin.

"Because you made them that way. You never tell them no, so they think they can do whatever they want."

"That's both of y'all," Nova said, looking up from her Kindle just long enough to glance at Logic and Joy. She was in one of the lounge chairs next to Nate with her leg thrown across his while he rubbed her thigh.

"Nope, that's all him. Whatever they want, they get," Joy said without hesitation.

"Yeah, aight, and who do they run to every time I say no? You, because you let them do what they want." Logic leaned over Joy so that he could see her face, which made her laugh because it was true. They were both suckers for their kids, but of the two, Joy was the weakest when it came to holding her ground with the twins.

"That's what I thought," Logic said just as Joy reached in the back pocket of her jeans and pulled her phone out. She hit ignore for the call and then frowned before sliding it back in her pocket.

"Your mom again?" Logic asked, leaning over her shoulder and kissing the side of her face. It pissed him off that Marilyn had the nerve to even attempt to contact Joy after all the bullshit she had done.

Joy nodded and covered his hands with hers. Joy and Logic had run into Joy's parents at a restaurant while they were out with the twins about a week ago. It had turned into a whole big thing with Logic on the verge of being arrested because he had decked Lionel when he tried to reach for LJ. Ever since then, Marilyn had been calling nonstop, begging to see the twins. She had apologized over and over again, but Joy wasn't trying to hear it. Logic didn't want Marilyn or Lionel anywhere near their kids, but even if he had been okay with it, it wouldn't have mattered anyway because Joy was over it. Her parents were dead to her and that wasn't changing. At some point, enough is enough.

"I'll change your number tomorrow." Logic whispered against her ear before kissing the side of her face again.

"Y'all some lazy ass kids, got me in here doing all the work while y'all out here doing nothing. Come eat, damn," Mini said, bursting through the back door.

"That's your fault. We tried to help, but you told us to get out of the kitchen," Nova said and rolled her eyes.

"That's because you can't cook. I was talking to Joy and Najah," Mini said and rolled her eyes, making Najah and Logic laugh.

"Come on, Ms. Mini. Don't do it like that. My baby can cook." Nate leaned toward Nova and kissed her cheek.

"Putting something in the microwave and pushing buttons is not cooking, little boy. I bet y'all eat out a lot, don't you?"

Nate laughed and Nova punched him in the arm, but it was true. Nova couldn't cook to save her life, but Nate didn't care. He loved her anyway, and if loving her meant carry out and restaurants then he was cool with that.

"Damn, Ma, that's cold," Logic said.

Mini just shook her head and stepped back in the house right before Gotti walked back up the stairs and sat down next to Najah. He leaned in to kiss her but she shoved him away and scrunched up her face because he was sweaty from shooting around with Trent.

"Would you move?" Najah looked up at him with a scowl.

"Aight, just remember that shit later." Gotti kissed her stomach and winked at her before he stood and leaned against the rail next to Logic. Najah shot him a bird.

"Your mean ass needs to hurry up and have that damn baby." Gotti returned the favor and shot her a bird.

"Don't be like that because that's all your fault with your nasty asses. I hate to even come to your house because I never know what I'm going to walk in on," Nova said.

"Yo, chill with all that. I damn sure don't want to hear that shit." Logic cut his eyes at Nova first and then his sister and Gotti.

"Man, whatever," Nova said and laughed, which made Gotti chuckle.

"You don't have no business at our house anyway. You need to have your ass at home in the kitchen trying to learn how to cook, so my man over there don't starve to death or go broke because of your non cooking ass." Gotti said.

"Kiss my ass, how about that?" Nova said.

"Nate, I hope you making six figures because you're gonna go broke just buying food and shit, fucking around with her." Logic pointed at Nova.

Nate chuckled and Nova grilled him with a murderous stare.

"Oh, so that's funny?" Nova said.

Now Nate was in full blown laughter.

"Man, let's go eat before y'all fuck around and have me in one of the guest rooms tonight."

"Nah, don't blame them, you're about to have yourself in one of the guest rooms with all that damn laughing you're doing," Nova said before she stood and pointed at Nate, who yanked her arm and pulled her into his lap.

"Don't front, you know that shit ain't happening." He kissed her on her on the neck, which made her smile.

"Yo, let's go eat. All y'all doing the most with that shit," Logic said, nudging Joy so he could move.

She laughed and caught his hand as they moved toward that back door. The rest followed, and everyone headed inside to eat. Family dinner had officially begun.

*****

Joy was finishing the last of the dishes while Logic was in the living room on the floor with the twins coloring. Leia on one side with LJ on the other. The house was finally empty, and Logic was happy just to chill with Joy and the twins for a minute. He loved his family and was more than happy to send them all home, because moments like this, when it was just him, Joy, and the twins was what he lived for.

Business was still going strong, but Logic and Gotti had finally gotten things to a point where they had good people in charge, so they spent very little time on the block. Although he still occasionally had a few late nights, it was rare. In fact, Logic had traded in time on the block for time with LJ and Leia. He had the them with him most of the time when they weren't with Mini, and he was perfectly content with that.

"Mommy, look, it's a flower." Leia held up the picture she had scribbled just as Joy positioned herself on Logic's back, leaned into him and placed her chin on his shoulder.

"That's perfect baby. Can I have it?"

Leia giggled and placed the paper back on the floor in front of her.

"I have to finish it first."

"You know you're heavy, right?" Logic teased, holding his head back just enough for Joy to plant a kiss on his lips.

"Shut up, no I'm not."

"Man, yes you are. I think you just broke my damn back."

"Mommy, don't break daddy's back, move." LJ jumped up and used his little hands to try and shove Joy off Logic's back, which made Logic laugh.

"I'm good, LJ, I was just playing, man."

LJ stood there with his arms folded and a scowl on his little face, like he was trying to decide if he believed his father or not. Joy smiled because he looked so much like Logic that it was funny. Especially with the expression he was sporting. LJ looked at Joy first and then Logic, and then just like that, he let it go and was on the floor, next to his father again coloring.

Joy shook her head and laughed. "That's your child."

"What?" Logic said with a smirk.

"You know what. You do no wrong in his eyes."

"Nah, that's you," Logic said, but he knew Joy was right.

LJ took his side no matter what. It was supposed to be mothers and sons, but in their case, LJ stayed up under Logic 24/7. He idolized his father and tried his best to imitate any and everything that Logic did, down to the cuss words that Logic had a hard time trying not to say. Joy was constantly on him about his language because if Logic said it, so did LJ.

"We both know better than that. I'm about to get them ready for bed. I'm tired and need to relax. Today was fun but exhausting."

"Nah, I got it. You go chill and I'll be in there in a few," Logic said.

Joy kissed the side of his face and smiled. He didn't have to tell her twice.

"That might have earned you some special privileges later."

"You know that's mine, right? I don't need your permission to be up in that," Logic said and pointed to her waist after she was on her feet again.

Joy laughed and rolled her eyes. "Come give me a hug, lady bug."

She opened her arms and Leia jumped up and ran into them. After a hug and a kiss, Joy said goodnight to her daughter and then walked over to LJ, who stayed put by his father's side. Joy leaned over and kissed him on the top of his head.

"Night, LJ."

"Night, Mommy," he said without moving or looking up at her. He was in the process of coloring the picture that Logic had in front of him. The two of them were in their own world, like they often were.

Joy left Logic and the twins and headed to their bedroom in dire need of a hot shower and their bed. Her first stop was the bathroom where she turned on the shower to let the water run hot and then back to the bedroom to get what she needed. After she had what she needed, she was in the bathroom again staring at her image in the mirror as she shed her clothes.

She smiled when her eyes scanned her stomach. Joy turned sideways, trying to get a better view, but there weren't any signs yet of their new addition. She had taken a pregnancy test earlier that morning after Mini had insisted yet again that she was pregnant. This time Joy had an idea she was, but Mini saying it forced her to take the test to be sure.

Once she was done with her shower, she climbed in bed and pulled the covers up over her shoulders. Not realizing how tired she really was, she dozed off immediately. Joy didn't wake up again until she felt Logic's body move next to hers and his kisses on her neck and shoulder.

"I take it you didn't have willing participants for bedtime," Joy said as she turned her body to face him.

"Man, no. Daddy, read this, Daddy just lay with me, Daddy it's dark, Daddy I'm scared." Logic went through the list of things that had held him up.

Joy laughed, knowing from experience just how good the twins were about squeezing extra time out of them before bedtime.

"You love it, though." She watched the smile spread across his face.

"Wouldn't trade it for the world," he said and kissed her lips.

"It's gonna really suck when you have to get all three of them to go to sleep."

Logic lifted his head and held it back just a little. "Three?"

Joy nodded and grinned.

"Yo, you serious?"

"You okay with that?" Joy asked.

"Fuck yeah. Shit, you can have ten more if you want."

"How about just this one and then we're done?" Joy said with a smug grin.

"No promises on that. You know I love you, right?"

"You better. I'm about to go through another nine months of torture because of you."

Logic offered up a cocky grin. "I didn't do that shit all by myself. You were there too, but you know I got you."

"You better. I hate this part," Joy whined.

"You'll be fine, just take care of my shorty in there."

"See, you're starting already. It's not even about me. It's all about the baby."

Logic burst out laughing. "Man, chill. It's always about you."

He grinned before he kissed Joy and pulled her into his body. It was true. It was all about her, and that baby was a part of her, so he had them both. Nothing was going to change that. Never in a million years would he have imagined his life to turn out the way it had. He was a husband and a father. Everything about his life began and ended with them. His family was his world and there was no question or doubt about where his loyalties lie.

**Join our mailing list to get a notification when Leo Sullivan Presents has another release!**

**Text LEOSULLIVAN to 22828 to join!**

**To submit a manuscript for our review, email us at leosullivanpresents@gmail.com**

CPSIA information can be obtained
at www.ICGtesting.com
Printed in the USA
LVOW04s1711261016

510385LV00011B/1096/P